THE DNA OF YOU AND ME

THE DNA OF YOU AND ME

A NOVEL

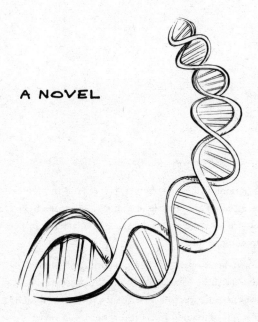

ANDREA ROTHMAN

WILLIAM MORROW
An Imprint of HarperCollins*Publishers*

HarperCollins books may be purchased for educational, business, or sales promotional use. For information, please email the Special Markets Department at SPsales@harpercollins.com.

FIRST EDITION

Designed by William Ruoto

DNA chain courtesy of Shutterstock/ArtMari

Library of Congress Cataloging-in-Publication Data has been applied for.

ISBN 978-0-06-285781-1

19 20 21 22 23 LSC 10 9 8 7 6 5 4 3 2 1

TO LARRY, ALEX, AND NATASHA

THE DNA OF YOU AND ME

PART ONE

THE WRONG GENES

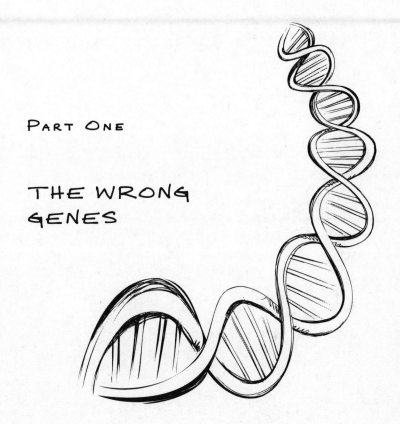

CHAPTER 1

*S*mell is an illusion, MY FATHER USED TO TELL ME: IN-visible molecules in the air converted by my brain into cinnamon, cut grass, burning wood. Heat was a measure of receptors in my skin, and brown was not brown but a combination of light waves captured by cones in my eyes. The world as I knew it, as I felt it to be, was the result of my own personal experience, and so it was up to me to make the best of my understanding of it.

If it is true that things are what you make of them, it can be argued that it was I who got in the way of Aeden's research, his life, and not the other way around. After all, he had been in the lab for three years when I first set foot there. Three years is a grain of sand in a scientist's life, but when you've been working in someone else's lab for that long you begin to hunger, irrationally, for a breakthrough in your work: your modest but unquestionable contribution to human knowledge.

Tomorrow I will be receiving an award—an important one. This award marks in many ways the true beginning of my career, and a point of no return in my life, the one I sometimes fear will have me forever looking back. At least that is how it feels now, and how it felt then, when I first got the news last month.

Giovanna, a senior postdoc in my laboratory, was in my office. It was our last meeting before her analysis of the strain of olfactory-impaired mice she engineered. The phone on my desk was ringing. It had been ringing for a while. Giovanna raised her head from the X-ray film on her lap and looked at me with a questioning smile. The room, though fully lit, felt as dim as the inside of a cave. I stood up from the desk and walked around her, over to the window, and raised the blinds. The light pouring through the glass stung my eyes momentarily, until I was able to see it: the Hudson flowing like melted steel in the distance.

"You know what they're saying out there about you?" Giovanna said.

"No." I turned from the window, not wanting to comment.

Her eyes followed me across the room, back to my chair. On my desk the phone was blinking. "They're saying that it could be you this year. That's what people are saying, Emily."

I stretched my arm across the desk. Reluctantly Giovanna deposited her film in my hand. "Hazy," I said, holding it between us like a veil. "The bands of DNA are hardly distinguishable from background noise. You'll need to design a better probe, Giovanna."

"Please tell me you didn't hear what I just said."

"And if it is me," I said. "What about it?" The results were unambiguously clear, despite the background noise. All the genes in the cocktail had been integrated into the genome of her mice. As usual, I was being overly cautious.

"Don't pretend that you don't care, Emily. I know you care. *You know you care.*"

"How old are they?" I asked.

"Seriously?" Giovanna said. Her hand was casually resting on the sphere of her belly. "Should I remind you that if you win this award you could go on to receive the Nobel Prize?"

"I really couldn't care less about the award nomination," I said. "Now tell me, are your mice old enough to analyze?"

Giovanna gave me one of her sidelong looks of resignation and drew out a spreadsheet from her marble notebook. That must have been when the phone began to ring again. Not the landline on my desk, but the one inside the raincoat draped over my chair. It was actually barking, a feature I much prefer to any other kind of ringtone. I let it bark. Giovanna raised her head from her spreadsheet and stared at me. I looked away from her, back at the film, and would have probably let the phone go on barking had it not been for her pregnant frame suddenly looming over me.

"If you don't answer that, I will," she said.

I patted the raincoat pockets and found the phone and raised it to an ear. I knew it was the call I'd been looking forward to and dreading in equal measure for the last ten years. Even saying hello into the receiver I found it hard to suppress the tremor in my voice.

"Dr. Apell?" It was a woman's voice, her tone exceedingly polite.

"Yes. Speaking."

"Good morning, Dr. Apell. You have been selected to receive the Lasker Award in basic medical research for your contribution to neuroscience. The ceremony will be held in September . . ."

After the call ended I just sat there, staring at the film on my desk. The bands of DNA were swaying like ships in a storm. I made a fist with my left hand. The other hand was still holding on to the phone.

"What's wrong?" Giovanna asked me.

"That was the Lasker Foundation."

"Oh my God." She cupped her nose. "Oh. My. God."

I raised a hand to stop her from yelling but she already was, yelling and rushing out of the office with the wobbling gait I sometimes envy her for, suspecting as I do that I will never have children.

A moment later there was a piercing whistle outside my door, and after a while the sound of people flooding the hallway. That was when I stood up from my desk and left the room. On my way to the exit doors at the end of the hallway there was a sea of feet I was somehow able to weave my way through without tripping into anyone. When I raised my eyes from the floor I could see faces from distant labs moving toward mine. I flung the doors open, turned into the nearest elevator, and dove inside it, catching in the mirror, before the doors closed behind me, the department secretary's perplexed smile, and an unopened bottle of champagne in her hand.

———

OUT ON THE STREET A MUTED RAIN WAS BEATING THE PAVEMENT. I pushed through the revolving doors of the building, past the institute's blue awning, and walked for several blocks without any particular aim. It took me a while to realize I had left my raincoat behind in the office and was soaked through, a while longer to recognize that I'd been walking east all along, toward the old campus.

At the university entrance a man in a khaki uniform eyed

me suspiciously from the guard booth. I was prepared to invent some story about having an appointment with Justin McKinnon, but he made no move to stop me from going through the gates.

Climbing the stairs up to the floor of the lab, I heard the sound of drilling, and smelled burnt rubber. The hallway, when I reached the top of the stairs, was hazed in dust, and looked to be considerably narrower than I remembered it. In the main room, from which all the noise seemed to be coming, the workbenches had been gutted. In their place small cubicles were being erected, approximately six cubicles per bay, the combined areas of which seemed somehow to fall short of the original space—as if it had shrunk with time. Even the aisle that cut across the room was significantly shorter in real life than the infinitely long and protracted one of my memory. I inched farther down the hallway, toward Justin's office.

The MCKINNON LABORATORY plaque was still there, fixed to the door with nails, but the frosted pane that had set Justin's door apart was coated in grime. I stood outside, thinking. Or rather, trying to make up my mind. I hadn't been back to the lab in nearly a decade; had avoided the campus, and running into Justin, like the plague. But now that I was there I would at least say hello to him and mention the news, which he would find out about sooner or later. I knocked on the pane and waited. No one answered. I rubbed an opening across the grime with the heel of my hand and was pressing my face to the glass, trying in vain to see through it, when a man opened the door from inside.

He was young, about thirty or so, with tousled red hair, and casually dressed in sweatpants and a T-shirt. The anteroom behind him was crammed with lab equipment, and sitting at the desk where Justin's secretary had sat was a young woman, her dark hair pinned to the crown of her head, her face leaning into a microscope. The little girl beside her was building a tower out of biological slides. She looked at me and I realized she was the daughter of the man standing in front of me, and that they were a family.

"Is Justin here?" I asked.

"Justin?" the young man said.

"Isn't this the McKinnon Lab?"

"Not anymore." He tightened his grip on the door handle. "I'm the new lab head."

"I don't understand," I said, though I probably did, at that point, understand.

"Justin McKinnon closed up shop last month."

"Justin retired?"

"I'm afraid so."

I folded my arms across my waterlogged dress, allowing the information to sink in. Justin retired at age fifty. Justin, whose life had revolved around the lab. What would he do with himself for the next twenty or thirty years, or however long he had to live? A chill was starting to seep into my bones.

"May I ask who you are?" the young man asked me.

The little girl's glass tower had collapsed. "Emily," I offered. "Emily Apell."

"Apell?" he said, looking closely at me. I held his gaze unblinkingly, and saw a spark of awareness register behind his clouded smile. "The same Apell who discovered that family of genes?" He snapped his fingers in the air. "What are they called?"

"Pathfinders," I said.

"Yes." He held out his hand to mine and I shook it. "Pathfinders," he repeated, looking both impressed and disoriented.

The woman behind him had risen from her chair. "Come inside and have some tea with us. You look like you're freezing to death."

The young man was holding the door wide open for me to step inside. The two of them were smiling at me from ear to ear. I wondered if they knew about the award, but of course they didn't. It would take several weeks for the Lasker winners to be announced, my name broadcast nationwide, on radio and television and the web. Their smiles, I was grateful to realize, had nothing to do with the award, and all to do with the discovery itself.

The rest of that morning I sat in the campus cafeteria with a cup of coffee, watching the thinning rain descend upon the East River, and it's where I've been coming to since, for nearly a month now. Especially with the developments of recent days, and the impending awards ceremony, I often find myself wanting to be alone, in a place where no one will know or remember me. After two o'clock in the afternoon there's hardly anyone here. I sit at a table by a window and stare out across the glass for hours, allowing my thoughts to come and go. But today I begin trying to put those thoughts together and in order, as if the past were some very long and misrouted nerve ending whose folds and kinks I'm untangling, straightening out so that it might find its proper path, the one it strayed from long ago.

I do it for Aeden. Mainly, though, I do it for me.

CHAPTER 2

THAT CRISP SEPTEMBER MORNING WHEN I FIRST arrived in the lab, fresh from graduate school, was twelve years ago now.

Justin led me past the trafficked hallway into a cavernous room with an unbroken view of the Queensboro Bridge and bays running the length of a sun-doused aisle like rows in an airplane. In every bay white-coated men and women around my age were absorbed in some task or other—or not absorbed at all. Some of them looked up to watch me move past them along the aisle in my outmoded jeans and tangerine sweater and a pair of knee-high boots whose flat soles, I realized with a knot in my stomach, only accentuated my meager height.

I steadied my dangling laptop on a hip bone and tried to make eye contact with everyone, and to smile, stopping wherever Justin stopped and opening my hand to whomever he saw fit to introduce me to: David Hobbs, Steven Kane, Eduardo Campos, Haru Oshiro, Mary Goodman, Wendy Nguyen . . . I matched their names to those in the bylines of the research papers from the lab that I'd read, and when memory failed me I attempted to figure out their status in the lab according to their appearance, guessing the fresh-faced people to be graduate students and the others, those with the complicated smiles and lines indented on their foreheads, to be the postdocs whose surnames had headed the grander papers.

By the time we'd reached the final stretch of the room I was perspiring from the effort of having to smile at people I didn't know, and uncomfortably aware of the buttery odor exuding from my scalp. I was relieved to make out the empty bay at the end of the room where I would be sitting: meant for only one person, instead of the usual two. We were about to reach it when Justin stopped in his tracks in front of the neighboring bay. A tall man stood there, his shoulders slouched, pouring DNA into the wells of a gel. We were standing only inches away from him, but it wasn't until Justin cleared his throat that he acknowledged us, and even then he was slow to react, slow to rise to his full height and turn his eyes to us.

"This is Emily Apell," Justin told him. "Your new neighbor."

Aeden brushed a hand against his faded jeans and, looking at me, allowing just enough time for his eyes to lock with mine in a kind of forced welcoming, shook my hand. "Aeden Doherty. Nice meeting you, Emily." Without another word he retook his multichannel pipette and went back to filling the wells of his gel.

Behind him, framed against the sunlit windowpane of their shared bay, a pretty brunette was sitting at a desk with a hardcover notebook opened across her lap. Her face was steadied on mine but when I made a point of meeting her eyes she stared down, at the notebook.

"Allegra Meltzer," Justin said, and to Allegra: "Allegra, this is Emily."

Allegra raised her large green eyes to mine, nodded, and looked back down.

It wasn't exactly a welcome party, and though neither Doherty nor Meltzer rang a bell, I imagined they were senior postdocs, with projects that were going somewhere, not interested in a newcomer like me. Yet I kept hoping, after Justin had seen me to my bay and rushed off saying he needed to be somewhere, that they would approach me to inquire what I was doing in the lab, and maybe even ask me to join them for lunch. Why not?

As a graduate student in Champaign, Illinois, I had identified three new members of a well-known family of genes involved in anticancer drug resistance, a study that had led to a respectable publication in a specialized journal for cancer research. It wasn't the sort of journal one might find in an airport terminal, on the shelves of Hudson News: not *Scientific American,* or the high-profile *Science* or *Nature,* where people in Justin's lab usually published their work. But then, I wasn't the kind of hands-on scientist they were, the kind of scientist one encountered in most labs back then. I was a bioinformatician. I used computers to analyze and interpret the biology encoded in DNA, and liked to think of myself as a sort of Watson-and-Crick of the new millennium.

Though what I wanted, what I was really looking for, I suppose, was to feel that I was one of them, one of the confident scientists in Justin's flashy lab, instead of the person in the small and obscure research lab I'd been a week ago.

And so when Aeden appeared at the foot of my bay sometime around noon and asked me if I'd had anything to eat, I immediately stood up from my desk, as if I'd been expecting him.

FIVE MINUTES LATER WE WERE HEADED ALONG A PATH OF IVORY
slabs bordered by tall research buildings and young maples, toward the cafeteria. The leaves of the trees were still green, despite it being late September and technically fall. The sky above
was cloudless and deep blue, the air brisk and smooth. Aeden
was staring fixedly ahead.

There was a complicated intensity about his face, a general
detachment in his manner with me that made me feel strangely
at a loss. I noticed the timer clipped to his pullover and wondered
if he'd left an experiment running in the lab.

We were nearing the wide quadrangle of buildings at the end
of the path when I recalled seeing Doherty and Meltzer in two
very technical and low-profile papers from the lab, which I had
followed with difficulty, not having any hands-on experience
manipulating genes. "I read your two papers," I said. "I think
they're awesome."

Aeden shot me a bloodless look. "Oh, please," he said, matter-
of-factly. I could smell nicotine on his breath. "It's just a load of
technical crap."

"The kind everyone in the field should be familiar with," I
said sincerely.

"How do you like it here?" he asked me, changing the subject.

"The campus?"

"New York."

"I just got here. This morning, actually."

He looked at me closely, holding me in his light gray eyes for
a long moment, as though he were seeing me for the first time.
"You came straight to the lab?"

I searched his face for the unfavorable opinion his even tone had not conveyed, and did not find it, or any other opinion. Unlike most people I'd met, he wasn't judging me. "I was anxious to get to work," I said, then, wanting to explain myself further, "The DNA database is the reason I came here, to this lab."

Aeden gave a slight shrug. He didn't bother to inquire what exactly about the database had brought me to the lab. His eyes were no longer even on me. The place we were headed to was visible in the distance, and his gaze was stubbornly anchored on it.

I wondered why he'd asked me to lunch, but didn't ask him. Or rather, chose not to. If there was an ulterior motive behind his invitation I didn't want to know about it.

The cafeteria at AUSR (American University of Science Research) was a one-story structure poised like a melting icicle at the edge of the East River. From a distance the roof looked almost deformed, until gradually the shape of a spiral staircase began to emerge, and on closer inspection the two helices of a molecule of DNA, bound by slabs of glass. Inside, the seating area was magnificently large, with carpeted floors and floor-to-ceiling windows looking out at the watchtowers of the Queensboro Bridge: oxidized little fortresses I imagined inhabited by an insane person with nowhere else to go.

Aeden led me past the cash register to a small table in a corner of the crowded dining hall. Penetrating odors wafted into the air, and people sat noisily chitchatting. Following him between the rows of tables I saw Steven and Eduardo from the lab. They had been lost in conversation until they spotted me moving past them with my tray of food, at which point they quit talking to each other and stared up at me. Men rarely noticed me, and I wondered why they had.

At the table Aeden poured two packs of sugar into his black

coffee and stirred it with a thin plastic straw. Ignoring the sealed sandwich on his tray, he raised the Styrofoam cup of coffee to his mouth, then lowered it back down.

"I know why you're here, Emily," he said. "Everyone does."

I dug my fork into my Cobb salad. "Really?" Despite the seriousness of his face I could feel a smile spreading across my own. I wanted to be taken seriously by my peers in the lab, wanted them to think I had potential.

"Justin told us about you. He held a group meeting last month to discuss the recent outpour of genomic data, the thousands of genes whose function no one knows anything about, just sitting there in public databases across the world. How important it was to bring someone like you to the lab, with your expertise in bioinformatics. How he'd already hired you, in fact."

"You don't sound too thrilled," I said, which he didn't. I felt my smile fading.

"In principle I'm not opposed to you perusing the database. I just think your talent would be put to better use researching something else."

I put down my fork. "What do you mean?"

Aeden slid his tray to one side and leaned into the table. "Allegra and I identified a set of promising genes. It's what we've been working on for the last three years."

The whole mess was descending on me like a dark cloud, and yet outside, beyond the windowpane, the day stood perfectly clear. Unable to hold his gaze any longer, I looked at his forehead, wedged with nascent wrinkles. "How do you know they're important?"

"We don't," Aeden said. "We don't have knockout mice to prove it, but we'll have them very soon."

"If you don't have the mice," I said, "you can't possibly know that your genes are doing what you think they're doing."

Aeden studied me across the table. The expression on his face was one of quiet amusement, or outright disbelief; it was difficult to say which, and the difference hardly seemed to matter. "I think you're missing the point here, Emily. The project is ours. It always was, from the beginning."

I didn't budge. Despite his territorial grab, or because of it, I had a feeling that he was scared. "Then why did Justin hire me?"

"*Justin?*" Aeden said, so incredulously that for a moment I wondered if we were talking about the same person. "Justin has nothing to lose. He only stands to win from having postdocs compete against each other in his lab. Whereas you, Allegra, me . . ." His hand went to his heart. For a moment I felt I knew what he was getting at: the dearth of jobs in academia, the struggle to stay, to find a niche. But what he said instead was: "This project is very important to me, Emily."

"And to me it isn't?" I managed to say.

"I'm not saying it's not. I'm sure it is. Look." His timer was beeping. "I hate to be the bearer of bad news. I know this can't be easy for you, your first day here, but I wanted to get it out of the way." Suddenly he was standing. "I'm sorry, I need to get back to the lab." He picked up the untouched sandwich on his tray.

"I appreciate your honesty about the project," I said stiffly. I couldn't look at him.

Aeden didn't move. I could feel him standing over me, watching me, until at last he stepped away from the table, leaving a faint smell of cigarette behind.

Somewhere outside I could hear the sound of a blowing horn, and when I turned to look out the window I saw a freight ship moving down the East River. The deck was crammed with containers, stacked one on top of the other in multicolored towers: black-green-orange-red . . . green-red-orange . . . red-red-green . . . yellow-black . . . There was no pattern to the sequence in which they were stacked, only a haphazard randomness I tried in vain to piece together, as if a color-coded motif could help me decide what to do: whether to stay in the lab or to leave.

The ship was already a spot in the distance when I pictured myself standing on its sunny deck, between the towers of containers, leaving the lab and what I'd gone there to do forever behind me. Imagining this I felt a tingle of liberation spreading throughout my body, radiating like heat from the soles of my feet to the crown of my head, and when that feeling died out—and it did very quickly—it was replaced by sheer terror.

Damn you, Justin, I thought.

Someone at a table nearby was laughing, and I was certain it was at me.

———

JUSTIN, WHEN I BARGED PAST HIS SECRETARY, WAS SITTING AT HIS desk chair with his back to the poster on the wall—a white-and-blue sphere riddled with wire-thin filaments converging on distinct destinations, like routes on an airline map. The sphere was a blown-up image of the forebrain of a mouse, and the filaments were nerve endings called axons. Neurons in the snout bearing more than a thousand types of odorant receptors projected their axons to as many targets in the brain. My job, the reason I had come to his lab, was to find out what guided them.

Justin raised his face calmly from the glow of his desktop screen, readjusting his spectacles over the bridge of his nose. He was wearing a starched white shirt and a blazer. "What can I do for you, Emily?"

I was standing practically over his desk, with my hands on my hips. "You never told me the project was taken."

"That's right. I was going to talk to you about that."

"Really? When?"

He pointed to the makeshift living room where we'd sat earlier in the day: me on the black leather couch and Justin in his wing-backed chair, stacks of *Nature* and *Science* journals piled on the coffee table between us and plush carpeting under our feet. "Please take a seat."

I shook my head emphatically. "Had I known this I would have never set foot in this lab."

Justin smiled at me. It was as if a wall between us had been breached, and he was enjoying the view. "And why is that?"

"Because what you're doing is unethical, that's why."

We had met months earlier, at a neuroscience conference in Chicago. I had approached the crowded refreshments table where Justin had been standing alone after his keynote speech, and inquired about an opening in his lab. Justin casually referred to an existing waiting list and stared back down at his BlackBerry. Stalling for time, I lifted a heavy thermos off the table and poured myself a coffee and forced myself to drink it. Justin hadn't moved. Not knowing what else to say to him, but feeling that I needed to make one more effort to stand out, I told him I was from Rockford. "That's west of here," I said. "Northwest, to be specific."

Justin looked up at me. I was expecting him to tell me to get lost, but he didn't. The directional detail for some reason touched a nerve. Before I knew it he was talking to me about the arctic winds in the Midwest and the bleak winter forecast for the following year, and also complaining bitterly about the bed in his room. The hotel manager ("a tall blond woman, very striking") had promised to replace his mattress with a firmer one. His coccyx was killing him, literally killing him.

I suggested that he take an Advil. I also agreed that the conference could have been better planned, and laughed profusely at his comment about the coffee at the table being so diluted it tasted like fish piss. In the breathing spaces of the conversation I filled him in on what I'd done in Vincent's lab at Urbana-Champaign and what I hoped to do in his: the group of genes that I hoped to uncover, waiting list allowing.

Six months later I received an email from him. A bay in his lab had been vacated and he looked forward to seeing me again in the near future. It took me less than a month to wrap up my graduate and undergraduate research in Champaign, dismantle my dorm life of nearly ten years, and drag my belongings halfway across the country, to Justin's lab.

"Unethical?" Justin repeated. "What about fair to science, Emily?"

The room was stuffy. Heavy traffic was inching mutely along the upper deck of the bridge outside the two windows. Like most lab windows, they were hermetically sealed, so I could hear no sound other than Justin's voice and the tapping of fingers on a keyboard outside the open door behind me.

Justin swiveled his chair around to face the poster on the wall. "No one in the world knows exactly how this happens," he said, circling the targets on the map with his hand. "No one really knows how the map of smell is formed."

"Aeden and Allegra will soon. They're light-years ahead of me."

"What if their genes have no role in guiding olfactory axons to their targets; have you thought of that?"

I sank into a metal folding chair in front of his desk. "And if they do," I said, "if the experiment with their mice is a success, I would be wasting my time here, wouldn't I?"

Justin stood up from the desk and hurried past me. "I'll be right back."

I could hear him behind me in the anteroom, talking to Karen, his secretary, and Karen saying, "Yes, of course. I'll let no one in." Then the door clicked shut, and Justin was back at his desk.

"Do you remember what you told me at the conference, back in March?"

I shook my head. "I said many things, Justin."

"This was personal."

"I don't remember," I said, though I did.

"You said that to find these genes was what you'd been born to do."

I folded my arms around my chest and shifted in my chair, aiming for a position that would make me feel less exposed and finding none. "I should never have said that."

"But you did," Justin said, almost effusively. "You did."

A crepuscular darkness had descended on the room, as if the day outside had been switched off. And there was something else in the room that I was just noticing, a scent that had probably been there all along, which I knew came from Justin, because I'd smelled it on him at the conference in Chicago, and earlier in the day, when I'd first arrived in the lab. It was a scent reminiscent of freshly laundered linens cooling off from the dryer, a smell I'd thought exclusive to my father and had been keenly aware of

during the last years of his life, whiffing it in the packages of vi-
tamin C he sometimes mailed me and during my weekend visits
to the house in Rockford. Particularly in winter, hanging my coat
in the small entrance closet where his own coat hung: that clean,
wide-open smell that now, after all these years, has come to feel
indefinably narrow.

"So what will it be?" Justin asked me, with an insinuating
smile. "Your best shot at it, or the Greyhound bus back to Champaign?"

I managed a smile. I hadn't gotten to New York by bus. I had
taken a direct flight from O'Hare, and he knew it. He also knew
that I was incapable of leaving. This was the fork in the road I'd
been headed to all my life, and like the neurons in the poster, I'd
already made my choice.

CHAPTER 3

IN THE BRAIN THERE'S A MAP OF SMELL. ODORS ARE represented in a pear-shaped structure behind the nose called the olfactory bulb, at spatially defined locations that light up in response to smoke, vanilla, grass . . . I knew this long before I read Justin's papers or heard his talk in Chicago, long before I ever stepped into a classroom.

As a child I was highly allergic to grass, in particular to cut grass, and so I spent summers indoors in my father's lab, or at home, leafing through the Girl Scouts magazines he encouraged me to read and gazing through the den window at mothers conversing amicably between mown lawns and kids shooting balls in the street and putting up lemonade stands in their front yards.

It wasn't something I necessarily wanted to do—put up a stand and shout at strangers passing by and pour lemonade into cups and gather the coins—but it was something I enjoyed watching the other kids do nonetheless. By age thirteen my body had become immune to the chemicals discharged in the air by cut grass, and yet the sweet iron odor of a sheared lawn still drove me indoors, and would continue to do so for many years, despite my father's relentless encouragement to step outside, ignore the smell—make an effort to befriend the neighborhood children I'd grown up with.

But we were no longer children, any of us, and at times it seemed to me that I was past getting to know them. Pedaling my bicycle at night to the local Hilander, where my father sent me to buy the milk and eggs we didn't need, I sometimes saw them, the teens my own age, sitting in a group by the wooden fence of our street with their cigarettes. If I waved at them, someone would usually wave back at me, and that was it, the extent of my interaction with them for a long time.

My persistent aversion to the smell of lawns, and by extension to civilization, was, according to my father, the reason that I had no friends, and he feared I would grow up to become a loner—which I did, in the end. If only because of this, smell was important to me.

That afternoon, after my conversation with Justin, I returned to the main room and picked up my laptop from my desk and walked back out again, through the nearest exit. In my dorm across the street I showered and unpacked my suitcase and opened the boxes I had shipped from Champaign, and surveyed an express delivery order from IKEA: a round wooden table with matching chairs, a sofa bed, a nightstand, scented candles for the bathroom, and a dinnerware set in the event that I had people over one evening.

Though I hardly saw myself entertaining, much less cooking, I still found pleasure imagining both. This was my first time in years with a kitchen all to myself, and a bed that didn't pop out of the wall. Compared to the dorms where I had lived since I'd left home, the one at AUSR was a luxury apartment, with windows above the radiator looking out at the East River promenade and smooth wooden floors on which the emptied cardboard boxes glided like felt.

Among the books and kitchen utensils and miscellaneous other objects I exhumed from the boxes I had packed after my father's death was a flower vase my mother had made with her own two hands and given him as a gift. My father had kept the vase up in our attic for years. Only after he retired did he take it down from its hiding place and stand it in the den, occasionally filling it with berry branches and flowers that grew wild in the forest behind our house.

My mother had worked for my father for two years as a research assistant in his lab before leaving chemistry altogether to do what she claimed she'd been born to do. She never told him exactly what that was, but according to my father it could have been anything from making pottery to waiting tables at IHOP.

They had a fling before she left. Twelve months later she appeared at his doorstep with a three-month-old baby and the threat of giving me up for adoption. My father took me in and raised me single-handedly, and that is all he ever told me about my mother. I never had a name or an address or a fingerprint, not even a picture of her face. Had I bumped into her on the street it would have been like bumping into a stranger. Had she come knocking on my door one day I would have been curious to meet her, but that would have been about it. My interest in my mother, for all the DNA we shared, never stretched much further than the one imaginary encounter: her knocking on my door and me opening it and seeing her, and slowly coming to recognize in her something about myself that I didn't quite know, or understand.

I untangled the vase from its plastic bubble shield and stood it at the center of the IKEA table. Warped triangles and crescent moons bulged abstractedly from its thin neck, like something made by either a professional artist or a preschooler. The base was a rusty orange color, the middle half a soothing lime green. My hands hovered uncertainly over the dark empty mouth of the neck, imagining flowers there. That is what my father would have wanted, and that is what I would do. As soon as I had the chance, I would buy flowers to put inside the vase, make this new apartment feel like home.

————

IT WAS LATE IN THE EVENING WHEN I RETURNED TO THE LAB, AND judging by people's reactions, I doubted that anyone was expecting to see me again that day, or any other. A cart loaded with empty mouse cages was blocking the entrance into the main room, and when I walked carefully around the cages with my laptop I saw Steven gazing at me with undisclosed interest, as if to say: *Look who's here.* David Hobbs, the lab technician, who was twenty-three years old but appeared to be closer to fourteen, was standing at the sink, filling an industrial beaker with distilled water. When I walked past him he smiled at me and raised a sympathetic hand in the air.

I could see Aeden two bays down, inserting vials into the DNA amplification machine on Allegra's bench. Of the two, she spotted me first, and nudged him in the ribs with her elbow. He stared up into the aisle, and for the instant that our eyes met I thought I sensed relief on his part to see me again, but I wasn't quite sure.

At my desk I hooked up my laptop to the lab's network and accessed the database. Justin had called it that, but in truth it was an unorganized and uncatalogued repository of gene fragments. There were close to a hundred files, and in each file were dozens of DNA sequences, most of them unnamed, like untold stories in a book.

I opened the first file in a long list and scrolled down to the nameless sequence I'd been browsing earlier in the day, which was spread across multiple lines. To find what I was looking for felt suddenly as close to impossible as identifying a rare bird in a forest from a fallen feather. But it *was* possible. Provided that the bird existed, if its feather was there, in the database, I would eventually find him.

I was copying the sequence on my screen into the window of a genomic database search engine when Aeden walked into my bay. "I'm glad you came back," he said.

"Are you?" I didn't look up, but I could see him from the corner of my eye, standing by the workbench with his thumbs hitched into his jeans pockets.

"When I mentioned that you could put your talent to better use I was referring to another project, not another lab. I never meant to suggest that you should leave this lab, Emily."

I looked at him. "That's good to know," I said without irony.

"Okay. I just wanted to make that clear."

"It's clear," I said, and shot him a reassuring smile. "Clear as daylight."

"We're ordering pizza for dinner," Aeden said. "If you want to join us in the conference room you're more than welcome."

But I could hardly see myself sitting with him and Allegra and the two other postdocs still in the lab, making small talk and having to pretend that nothing had happened. Or worse: feeling pressed to invent some story about how I was looking for something else to research.

"I already had dinner," I said, though I hadn't.

Aeden gave me a careful nod, not quite believing me. "If you change your mind, let me know."

"I will, thank you."

Leaving the lab several hours later I saw them sitting in the conference room, all four of them bunched at one end of the oval table: Aeden and Allegra on one side and Wendy and Steven on the other, leftover pizza on a paper plate and opened cans of Diet Coke between them. I could hear snippets of their conversation, the usual gossip that had circulated in my old lab about one lab scooping another, getting their work published first. Steven blurted some oblique comment about irreproducible data that I failed to catch. Everyone laughed, including Aeden.

I was about to step away from the door when Aeden caught sight of me through the pane. He made a motion to stand up, but before he could I turned around and walked quickly down the hallway, away from the conference room and out of the lab. The easy familiarity of the four reminded me for some reason of an incident from long ago that I thought I'd forgotten, but hadn't.

On my way back from the Hilander one evening I made the split-second decision to join the kids from my street, several of whom were my classmates in school, though we'd rarely spoken. There was a warm, pleasant breeze and the moon was full, and their voices were crisp and articulate in the calm night air. I got off my bicycle, parked it on the street, and went to sit down on the curb with them. At first they sort of froze, and there was an uncomfortable silence in the air. But very quickly they picked up where they'd left off. I sat at the edge of the circle, with my knees pressed to my chest, waiting for someone to talk to me, but no one did. I racked my brain for something to say, and found that I had nothing that I thought they might want to hear—nothing about the bands they listened to or the dwindling black market where they got their cigarettes, or about how they would have to put up with their parents for another three years before they saw freedom. And I felt, moreover, that even if I'd said something that was of interest to them, it wouldn't make a difference. The void between us, between myself and other people, was unbridgeable. At a break in their conversation, before I could be embarrassed any further, I stood up and got back on the bicycle. But as I pedaled away, relieved, I felt a door closing behind me forever.

CHAPTER 4

A FEW DAYS AFTER MY ARRIVAL IN THE LAB, I walked into the main room early one morning to see Aeden and Allegra extracting vials from the PCR machine.

From my desk I watched Aeden pipette the contents of the vials into the wells of the gel on his bench. It was what he'd been doing when I'd first met him, and practically all week. But something about the tender care with which he was loading these particular samples, as if he feared to lose even a single drop, told me they were different, and possibly special: the culmination of something rather than the beginning.

Half an hour later Aeden was carrying the gel tray to the Eagle Eye across my bay, Allegra skidding in her heels behind him, her long dark hair held to the crown of her head by a dangling barrette. Aeden slid the gel into the machine and angled the screen toward them. The screen lit up, and I saw the columns of bands glowing against the black backdrop, and then I understood: the DNA on the screen belonged to their mutant mice.

Allegra was jumping up and down, like a child. "Knockouts. We have knockout mice." Aeden lifted her off the floor and whirled her around in circles until they fell into each other's arms, laughing nervously, like the sole survivors of some huge catastrophe.

I suppose I should have been happy for them, and relieved to know that within a couple of weeks, or however long it took them to analyze their knockouts, I would know if the genes they had identified and deleted were important, and possibly the same ones I was looking to find. But I was horror-struck by the speed at which things were unfolding, the way time seemed to be closing in on me.

Aeden and Allegra returned to their bay and stood at her desk examining snapshots of their DNA. Unable to work, I sat senselessly observing Allegra's hair, now spread like a shawl across her back: how certain browns, glistening in the sun, gave off a reddish hue similar to the color of my own hair. I waited for someone else to show up, so that in the diversion created by his or her arrival I might walk out unnoticed, until it dawned on me that it was Saturday, and that no one would be showing up in the lab anytime soon.

Slowly, I stood up from my desk and got into my coat—a red windbreaker my father had gotten me for Christmas long ago. I was halfway out of the bay when I spotted something glinting in the aisle: Allegra's hairclip. I raked it off the linoleum, slipped it into my coat pocket, and kept walking.

———

OUTSIDE I MOVED NORTH, TOWARD THE WROUGHT-IRON GATES OF the campus, feeling like a thief with Allegra's hairclip in my pocket and at the same time strangely avenged. On the street I crossed the avenue and headed west, past First and Second Avenues into Third, Lexington, and Park, venturing into areas of the city I'd never seen before. The day was cold and metallically luminous, the sky seamlessly blue. I walked fast, as though running away from something.

Until somewhere along Madison Avenue, feeling out of breath and so parched it hurt to swallow, I walked into a diner called Nectar. Averting my eyes from the two crowded rows of booths on either side of the entrance, I scurried to the no-less-crowded counter at the edge of the room and found a stool sandwiched between two strangers. A woman with graying red hair and freckles on her face was working the counter. I ordered poached eggs and a coffee, and when the coffee came I wrapped my hands around the mug, glad of the warmth.

"You okay, honey?" the woman behind the counter asked me in a Slavic accent. Her name tag read GALINA.

"I'm fine, thank you," I said, not wanting to start a conversation.

"You sure?"

"Yes," I said, as graciously as I could. For all I knew she could have been my mother. Any stranger with a slight resemblance to me could have been my mother.

The eggs, when they arrived, were too runny for my liking.

"What's the matter?" Galina asked, seeing me put my spoon down.

"They're undercooked."

She whisked the little bowl away and returned it a few minutes later, the bracelets on her wrist clanking hollowly. "There you go."

But the yolks were now overcooked.

"Still no good, honey?"

The look on her face made me wonder if she thought I was about to start crying. "They're perfect," I said.

After she was gone I dipped a hand into my coat pocket and laid Allegra's hairclip on the countertop. And then I confronted what bothered me: their imminent results, which I had no way of foreseeing. But also how Aeden had swept Allegra off her feet and whirled her around, so spontaneously.

The last person I'd gone out with, a particle physics student from a neighboring lab in Champaign, had smiled politely when I'd tried to make a joke, and said I had an unusual hair color. "Like it's on fire or something," he'd observed across the table. I'd cut the date short, and we did not see each other again. My joke—about a mutant egg coming before the chicken—was lame, admittedly. But the bigger picture had gone through him like a quark, and what did the color of my hair have to do with anything?

I stood up from the bar stool, asked Galina for the check, and went to pay up front, leaving her the most generous tip I could afford and Allegra's hairclip lying on the counter.

———

WHEN I RETURNED TO THE LAB, JUSTIN WAS SITTING IN ALLEGRA'S desk chair. I hadn't spoken to him in days, and was surprised to see him there on a Saturday.

"Three weeks?" he said. "Why don't you analyze them now?"

"Mice aren't analyzed at birth," Aeden replied, sounding irritated. "Everyone in the field knows that, Justin."

"So what?" Justin shot back. "Where is it written you have to go by the book?" He watched me walk into my bay. All three of them did. I had reached my desk when Justin said, "At any rate, this certainly deserves a celebration. You guys up for brunch?"

Through the vertical aperture between our desks I watched Aeden pull his fleece sweatshirt over his head. Compared to Justin's woolen Ivy League sweater, the pullover looked worn and ratty, as though he might have slept in it. Allegra snatched her purse from her desk and lifted her fashionable coat off the backrest of her chair. I looked away as they left but only after I heard the doors flapping at the end of the hallway did I sink into my chair and access the database.

I can't say how long I'd been sitting with my face to the screen, a minute or two or twenty, when I felt a whiff of cold street air and heard a slight sound, so delicate it was as though someone were turning a page in a book. I looked up, and there was Aeden, standing next to me. "I didn't mean to startle you," he said, raising a hand.

"You didn't," I said, though I was, both startled and pleasantly surprised.

"I'm guessing you already heard about our mice."

"Yes. Congratulations."

Aeden pulled out the stool under my workbench and sat down on it. The sequence on my laptop was in plain sight on the screen, but he wasn't looking at it. "Aren't you supposed to be celebrating?" I asked him.

"I thought you might want to join us."

"Why?"

"It occurred to me that between the three of us we could help you brainstorm a new project."

"Justin agreed to this?" I couldn't imagine that.

"Is there a reason why he shouldn't?"

I shook my head. "No reason." I hesitated, and then said, "You don't have to be nice to me. There's really no need."

"I'm not trying to be nice," Aeden said. "I'm concerned about you."

"I'll take that as a compliment," I said.

Aeden smiled at me across the sunlit air. "So are you coming or not?"

I wondered what, if anything, he saw when he looked at me: small nail-bitten hands and limp red hair, a lightly freckled nose on a face that was pretty enough? But that wasn't all there was to see, or couldn't he tell? Couldn't he see that I wasn't about to give up on the project? "I'm not," I said. "I appreciate your concern for me, Aeden, but I think I'm capable of finding my own way."

Aeden raised an eyebrow at me. "Fair enough," he said, and stood up.

He was walking away when I heard myself say, "Thank you for thinking of me."

"You're welcome," he said.

CHAPTER 5

A GENE IS A STORY, WITH A BEGINNING, MIDDLE, and end. It is a long and finite sequence of DNA made up of ATGC nucleotides. The beginning of every gene is ATG, the universal ending TAG, or TAA, or TGA. But what lies in between the beginning and the end is different for each gene, and encoded in these differences are protein molecules with wide-ranging functions.

Unraveling on my laptop screen from morning to night were sequences whose nucleotides appeared to have fallen randomly in place:

ACTTTTGTACCTTTCTCGCCGGGACAGAGAAGTGGG-
CCGGGACCAGCCGGGCCAGACCAGACTGGACCCCAG-
GGGCGATGCGGCTGCTGCCCCTGCTGCGGACTGT-
GCTCTGGGCCGCGCTGCTCGGCT . . .

But nothing was random. There was music in the white noise, and it was my job to find it. Day after day I watched sequence fragments unfurling on my screen; day after day I sat at my desk assembling and reconstructing them to their full

length, comparing them to gene sequences in public databases and assigning them names and functions, weeding out
redundant genes and analyzing prime candidates: unknown
sequences that encoded axon guidance proteins.

David Hobbs, as it turned out, had made the database. He
had started out by building a library of bacteria carrying genes
expressed in the mouse olfactory bulb. Hundreds of bacterial
colonies from the library had been randomly selected, and
their mouse DNA sequenced and uploaded into files. Most of
the sequences, the ones I had examined, encoded housekeeping proteins. Only a handful encoded axon guidance proteins,
and they were not novel; they were genes whose function in the
bulb had been tested, and they did not explain how olfactory
nerves, hundreds of thousands possessing different odorant
receptor types, ultimately reached their targets, allowing us to
smell.

I wanted to believe that the gene I was looking for was in
the database, and that it would eventually make its appearance.
When it happened, I told myself, when the sequence popped
up on my screen, I would recognize it, in all its nuanced glory.
But the truth was that of the many genes I had annotated, very
few were novel, and of these none encoded an axon guidance
protein. I was nowhere near done with the database, but the
more sequences I sifted through, the more unlikely it felt that
I would ever come across what I was looking to find, and the
more plausible it seemed that Aeden and Allegra had already
found it.

Hearing them discuss their data from my desk, I often
wondered how they'd come upon their genes—the ones they'd

knocked out of the mice they were waiting to analyze. I had read about techniques devised to hook genes from commercial libraries to specially designed probes, like one might hook fish to bait. Most of them weren't subtle enough to pick up rare genes. But then I didn't know what Aeden and Allegra had picked up, and as the weeks rolled by it became increasingly difficult for me to work, to keep my eyes on my screen instead of peering through the aperture of my desk into Aeden's bay, where a fat green folder he'd recently pulled out of his filing cabinet lay open.

Most of the pages in the folder were hand-drawn sketches of gene constructs resembling from afar the architectural blueprints of modern and beautifully elaborate houses. But among these loose and incomprehensible drawings were the printed copies of the three genes Aeden and Allegra had knocked out of their mice. Despite knowing that I shouldn't, I tried to make out the sequences from my desk, but the font was small, and accurately reading the ATGC letters was like trying to decipher a road sign from a mile away. Still, every day at noon, when Aeden usually returned to his desk with his lunch and sat at his chair to examine the printouts, I subtly slid to the edge of my swivel chair and strained my neck and eyes for a better view, at the risk of being seen by him.

One time I fell off my chair, tipping my mug of sharpened pencils along the way and causing such a racket that Aeden shot up from his desk. "Are you okay?" he asked, across a floating ledge of petri dishes.

"Fine," came my broken reply as I pulled myself up from the floor. "I'm fine."

But I wasn't fine at all.

On a rainy day in October, Aeden didn't return from the cafeteria as he usually did. Impatient and curious, I walked out into the hallway and saw him in the conference room, standing in front of the whiteboard with a blue marker, discussing his knockout experiment and what he hoped to find in his mice with several other postdocs from the lab. Outlined on the board was a Mickey Mouse head, dotted in red, and shooting up from its snout were long blue threads that failed to reach the red dots, instead wandering off on their own. It was a hypothetical result, but a dream one nonetheless. The kind of results that would mean that the genes they had identified were involved in directing the axons to their targets.

———

THE FOLLOWING DAY I MUSCLED MY WAY INTO JUSTIN'S OFFICE, not bothering to knock on his door for the second time in a row. He was standing in the anteroom with his wrists held out to Karen, who was helping him with his cuff links. The window slats were open, and the room was blindingly bright.

"Were there no doors in your old lab?" Justin asked.

I pulled the door shut, deflecting the noise of an industrial centrifuge. "I would like to see their genes," I said.

Justin looked at me. "Why?"

"I think I deserve to know what genes they knocked out, whether I'm searching for something they already found."

"I'm afraid I can't help you there," Justin said. He looked away again. "Aeden is very secretive about his work."

"Don't you have the printouts?"

"No, I don't. Aeden never gave them to me, and I never requested them."

"You can request them now," I said. "Can't you? He won't say
no to you."

Karen glanced over her shoulder at me.

"He will say no," Justin said. His eyes went down to Karen,
who was diligently attempting to slide the tiny silver mouse in
her hand through the buttonhole of his cuff. "And even if he said
yes, I see no point in it. They're analyzing their mice next week."

"Next week isn't nearly soon enough," I said.

Justin chuckled. "What would you like me to do, speed up
time?"

"There you go," Karen said, stepping away from him, toward
her desk. "Do you have your Altoids?"

Justin patted his breast pocket, then pulled out a small red tin
and popped several mints into his mouth. The scent of spearmint
reached me almost instantly, bringing with it a happy childhood
memory I couldn't quite place. Justin put the tin away, grabbed
his roll-on suitcase, and began to move toward me. According
to the email he'd recently sent to everyone, he was scheduled to
leave that morning for a conference on the West Coast.

"I would like to see their genes," I reminded him.

"Unfortunately it will have to wait until I return," Justin said,
averting his eyes.

"I would like to see them now. I should have asked to see them
my first day here. I don't know what I was thinking." I had in fact
thought of asking him for the printouts of Aeden and Allegra's
genes then, but hadn't summoned the nerve.

Justin stood gazing at me in that direct, almost childlike way of his. And there was that smell again: pressed linens and freshly laundered towels. Where was it lodged in him, this smell: in his lint-free suit, the patch of grays on the left side of his head, his freshly shaven face? Why did it make me trust him?

"I have a flight to catch, Emily."

I was standing with my back to the door, blocking his way out. "Their genes, Justin."

"I'm sure you'll come across them in the database."

"I have yet to find something useful in that database," I said, infuriated. "Allegra and Aeden's results will be published and I'll still be on my hands and knees, searching for the needle in the haystack."

Justin's gaze slipped down, landing awkwardly on my flat boots. His cheeks, I realized, were flushed red. "I never said it would be easy." He stepped around me and before I could say another word he'd slid past me with his roll-on.

The door slammed shut in my face and I heard a little snort behind me. I turned around to see Karen biting her lower lip. She pushed a silver strand of hair behind an ear and frowned into her computer screen, as if asking it about me: *What planet is she from?*

"You think I'm being unreasonable, Karen?" I asked. Though I knew the answer was yes, I still wanted it to be no.

Karen gave out a long breath. "It's not my job to judge you, or anyone else here," she said, glancing at the door through which Justin had escaped.

"What would you do if you were in my shoes?"

Karen hesitated. The tapping of her fingers on the keyboard had come to an end, leaving a silence in the room that felt almost soul searching. Then she said, "You're not the first person coming in here with a bone to pick with Justin. And you won't be the last. If I were you I would leave. I would find myself a less promising but kinder career path. Life is too short."

I nodded, agreeing that life was short. "Thank you," I said, and quietly let myself out the door.

CHAPTER 6

THE NIGHT BEFORE AEDEN AND ALLEGRA ANA-
lyzed their mice, Justin strode into the main
room of the lab looking restless and sleep deprived and also,
mysteriously, more fully alive than I'd ever seen him. It wasn't
yet midnight, but close, and the lab was so quiet that I could hear
the clock ticking on the wall and the echo of his footsteps trailing
behind him.

Aeden and I were alone in the room. He was installing a dissecting scope on his bench: a round-based stereoscope similar
to the one I'd used in my father's lab as a child to examine blades
of grass.

Justin plunked himself down on Allegra's empty desk chair.
"Guess who was at the conference in San Diego?"

"I have no clue," Aeden said, not looking at him.

"Craig Wallace, remember him?"

"How could I forget?"

"Guess who he's working for?"

Aeden shrugged.

"Take a wild guess."

"Is it important?"

"Carol Levine. Have you heard of her?"

Aeden shook his head, concentrating on the stereoscope eyepiece.

"She runs a fruit fly lab at the Salk Institute. They have a strain of mutant flies that die young. Apparently they have a hard time finding the food source in those tubes where they're bred."

"Something to do with smell loss, no doubt," Aeden said ironically.

"As a matter of fact it does," Justin said, crossing his legs. "Craig analyzed the dead flies, and their map of smell is in shambles. Not only that, but the mutated gene encodes a novel axon guidance protein."

"Any other information about the gene?" Aeden asked, turning away from his bench to face Justin.

"They didn't say. But after a few whiskeys on my tab at the hotel bar I got Craig talking, and guess what? Carol is planning to submit his results to *Science* next year."

After a pause, Aeden said, "I find that hard to believe."

"You think he's lying about the paper?"

"I find it hard to believe the map of smell is in shambles. He's probably just saying that to get back at you, after what happened to him here."

Justin ignored the comment. "In shambles or not, as soon as your results are ready we'll write up a paper and submit it to *Science*, before they do." He looked away from Aeden and straight at me, across the gap between Aeden's desk and mine. "How's that for a plan?"

"I wouldn't expect anything less of you," Aeden told him.

Justin giggled. I held my breath and watched him stand up from the chair. "I'm looking forward to tomorrow. I expect great things from you guys." Before I could count to ten he'd left the room and vanished into the hallway.

Without looking at Aeden, I stood up and followed Justin out. At the end of the hallway I could see his stout figure receding. "Justin," I called out, trying not to raise my voice. I knew he could hear me, but he didn't stop. When I caught up with him a moment later he was about to walk into an elevator. "Their genes," I said, intercepting him. "I need to analyze them. It will help us know what to expect of their results."

"All the information you need is in his filing cabinet," Justin said, maneuvering his way around me, into the waiting elevator.

"And what am I supposed to do, break into it?"

Justin smiled at me. "That's up to you," he said, and the elevator doors came sliding shut between us.

———

IN MY DORM I HAD A DINNER OF RAMEN NOODLES STRAIGHT OUT of the Styrofoam container, brushed my teeth, and changed out of my clothes into a pair of Gap pajamas. Lying on the sofa bed by the window I watched the headlights of cars from the FDR Drive skitter across the low popcorn ceiling, a strategy I'd been using lately to fall asleep, and allowed my thoughts to drift, as I sometimes did, to the day when Aeden had asked me across a ledge of petri dishes if I was okay. I felt his hand on my cheek, and the warmth of his breath on my throat. His mouth, light as a feather, was on my mouth, now on my nose, my eyes, my hair.

I awoke with a start. My bangs were plastered to my forehead with sweat, and my heart pounded under the light cotton fabric of my shirt. In just a few hours Aeden and Allegra would analyze their mice. A few hours more and I would know if their genes were the same ones I'd come to the lab to find. But a few hours may as well have been a lifetime away.

Without thinking about what I was doing, I put on jeans and a sweater and ran out the door. It was pouring rain outside, and I was instantly soaked. Half-blinded by the rain, I thought I saw a man standing on the opposite side of the street, and heard the faint barking of a dog—but when I squinted more closely there was no one there, nothing but a lamppost glowing weakly on a deserted sidewalk. A cold stream of water seeped into my shoes—an old pair of Converse sneakers—as I ran toward the tall research buildings of the AUSR campus. The guard at the entrance pressed his face to the streaming glass of his booth and rang me in, not bothering to inspect my identity card or to ask what I was doing there at three in the morning.

Upstairs, on the fifth floor, night lights illuminated the path from the elevator in the lobby to the main room, though I could have found my way there blindfolded. I let myself in through the farthest door, closest to Aeden's bay, locked the door behind me, and went to his workbench.

Silhouetted against the darkness I could see the dissecting scope Aeden had been calibrating, and the metallic sheen of the aluminum foil sheet beneath it, bearing scalpels and glass vials with screw-on caps, a dissecting kit, and an empty ice bucket. I moved up to his desk. A Starbucks cup with its sides all chewed up was pushed against the desk wall, alongside a series of papers on smell disorders I'd never read up on and knew nothing about: paranosmia, phantosmia, hyposmia, anosmia. In the air was an unsettling odor of tobacco, and something very faint, like sea breeze. Beneath the desk, next to the filing cabinet, a tennis racket lay exposed on the floor.

The filing cabinet was locked. I pulled open the desk drawer and saw there, among the loose coins and a pack of cigarettes, a silver set of keys.

Fastened to the cork of the desk wall were photographs of people, presumably friends and family. They gazed at me from bar stools and fireplaces, car windows and ski slopes, white-sanded beaches and mountains that seemed to touch the sky. In one of the pictures was a field of grass so green I wondered if it was even real. In another picture a middle-aged woman with gray eyes similar to Aeden's smiled quizzically, almost sadly, at me, as if imploring me to stop. But the keys were in my hand, and I was no longer standing, but on my knees, sifting through the sea of green folders in Aeden's filing cabinet.

At my desk I tried to ignore the jabbing pain in my head, and turned my face away from the picture on my own desk wall—a photograph of my father, taken when he was still setting up his chemistry lab: long-sleeved lab coat and clean-shaven face, shy blue eyes and a smile so wide and hopeful it was almost humbling.

I sank into my chair with the printouts of their three genes. One by one, I entered clips of the sequences into the window of a mouse genomic database, hit the Search tab, and watched links to matching sequences come up on my screen. Their genes were not new, as I had thought. They were known genes, and though their function in the olfactory bulb had not been tested, they belonged to a family of axon guidance molecules with well-documented functions in the brain. Moreover, a phylogenetic tree of the family showed that they were closely related to other gene members. This meant that if they had a role in the bulb, it was unlikely to be unique.

It also meant that they were probably not it: not the genes I was looking to find.

————

BY THE TIME I LEFT THE LAB THE SUN HAD RISEN, AND IT WAS NO longer raining. Brown leaves lay scattered across the campus grounds, all twisted and bent out of shape, but beautiful in their own way. The air was unexpectedly cold but had the pleasant smell of pencil shavings. I hurried toward the gates, and reached them to see Allegra descending a bus across the street. A chill coursed down my spine, a sense of being frozen in place, locked forever where I stood, at the foot of the gates in my damp clothing. Until she suddenly turned uptown, away from me, and I was able to breathe again. No one would ever know what I'd done, and no one had gotten hurt.

The sidewalk to the dorm building was speckled with sunlight and dotted with early risers. I saw women my age pushing babies in strollers, women clipping by in heels with their hair still wet from a shower. I saw men walking their kids to school with their phones held to their ears, and for some reason thought of Aeden. I remembered the lawn of grass on his desk wall, its freshness, and wished I could take back what I'd done.

CHAPTER 7

G ROWING UP I OFTEN ENCOUNTERED MICE IN our house, despite my father's efforts to keep the place clean. After dinner he would wander the small area of the kitchen with a rag over his shoulder and a cordless Black + Decker in his hand, swabbing the oil-splattered stove and running the vacuum over vegetable peels long adhered to the hardwood floor. My father was well over fifty and had lost his ability to see clearly without his glasses, and even with the glasses on, he was often too absorbed in his thoughts to give himself wholeheartedly to what he referred to as "the brain-cell-killing task of housekeeping." Consequently, mice roamed our kitchen freely at night, especially during winter: gray-coated field mice so plump and tiny and strangely alive they seemed to have stepped straight out of a Hans Christian Andersen fairy tale.

More often than not they sniffed their way into the pantry and ended up stuck there to one of my father's glue traps. Early the next day I would hear chirping sounds in the kitchen and run downstairs to find my father slouched over an old shoe box, syringing vegetable oil onto a squealing mouse's cemented feet, drop by drop.

While the procedure lasted, the tiny creature thrashed miserably in place, stirring a scent like sawdust into the air, until the glue holding its claws to the paper dissolved in the oil and the mouse was able to wiggle free. Week after week, year after year, I followed my father out the door, to the forest behind our home, and watched mouse after mouse spring out of the shoe box and dash across the snow. "So long, sucker," my father would yell after them, with his hand raised in a farewell salute. I laughed, watching him do that, though I was also saddened to imagine the mouse starving to death in some frigid hole in the ground, despite my father's words of reassurance that their coats were thick and well insulated and nature would provide for them one way or another. And anyhow, he said to me once, making purposeful eye contact, their sense of smell was ultimately powerful enough to steer them in the right direction.

The summer I was eight we had the kitchen baseboards replaced, and I didn't see a living mouse up close again until some twenty years later, when I walked into the main room that morning, two hours after returning the folder to Aeden's filing cabinet.

On his bench was a cage similar to the ones I'd seen David wheeling out of the lab. Huddled against the see-through plastic wall of the cage was a litter of mice: brown instead of gray, and easily twice the size of their brothers in the wild. Their coats shone in the sunlight, natural light they'd probably never seen or felt. Aeden sat slouched over the scope in his faded jeans and a black T-shirt, forceps in his left hand and surgical scissors in the other, skinning a small head on the lit stage of the scope with the mindless precision of a surgeon. Allegra stood next to him in her lab coat, oblivious to my presence at the door.

I walked quietly past them and went to sit at my desk. Every ten minutes I could hear the mice clawing at the walls of their cage, too smooth and even to hold any traction, followed by a rapid succession of squeals, and then that awful silence. Who knows what a mouse feels at the instant its spine is dislocated, what it continues to feel after its head is no longer attached to its body, the last smell it perceives?

Before I knew it the cage was empty, and the dimethylformamide of their neuron-staining solution had wafted into my bay, permeating the air with a stink similar to rotting fish. Through the gap between our bays I could see a rocker seesawing on Allegra's bench, and mounted on its base liquid-filled vials with tiny skull-like things drifting inside. I stared at the orphan gene on my screen and then shut my eyes.

Outside it was cold and windy but the sky was clear. I saw no trace of the fallen tree leaves of earlier, and wondered if someone had raked and bagged them away, or if the wind had simply dispersed them throughout campus. In the cafeteria I ordered a grilled cheese sandwich and a coffee and walked into the dining hall with my tray. I was about to make my way to an empty table in a corner of the room when I saw Aeden and Allegra sitting nearby, chatting serenely over breakfasts of eggs and bacon and coffee, like a married couple.

Before Aeden could see me I darted out of the hall, instead eating my sandwich on the roof terrace, staring at the East River flowing southward beneath me. For the next half hour I roamed the campus grounds, past research buildings and administrative buildings, the dome-shaped auditorium and the faculty club, the library and a small preschool that felt about as strange and unfamiliar to me as the dark side of the moon.

I walked a path lined with elms, up to a sad three-story structure without visible windows: the Animal Facility, where the
mice were housed. Here the path split in two: one leading into
the building and the other looping away, in the opposite direction. I took the second route, and made it back to the lab in
time to see Aeden and Allegra walking into the imaging room
with their data notebook and a bucket of ice containing their
vials.

When they returned to their bay, some four hours later, the
ice had melted and the vials were floating sideways in the water like shipwrecks. Aeden collapsed into his desk chair and sat
quietly, with his head in his hands. Beyond the window of his
desk was a pale strip of sky, the river beneath it coursing southward, toward the sunless watchtowers of the bridge. I had no way
of knowing what had transpired in the imaging room, what their
results were, and yet I knew.

Neither of them said a word until Steven barged into their
bay. "How did it go?" he asked.

"We don't know," Allegra said from her desk. There were dark
circles under her eyes.

"Bullshit," Steven said. "How could you not know?" He was a
big blue-eyed guy with a round teddy bear face, and also, as far as
I could tell, one of Aeden's trusted friends. "What's the verdict?"
he asked Aeden, settling a beefy hand on his shoulder.

"Do you mind if we talk later, Steven?" Aeden said, not meeting his eyes.

"Seriously?" Steven said, and with a hearty laugh, "The results are that bad, huh?"

Then Aeden did stare up at him. "They're not bad. They're
just difficult to interpret."

———————

COMING INTO THE LAB THREE DAYS LATER I SAW A CART LADEN
with empty mouse cages parked on the far side of the hallway,
near the main room entrance closest to Aeden and Allegra's bay.
I was already used to the sight, and would have thought nothing
of it had it not been for the fact that the door to Justin's office,
perpetually shut, was wide open, and the hallway itself, normally
bustling with activity at that hour of the morning, was eerily
quiet. When I walked into the room, Justin was standing over
Aeden and Allegra, swinging his arms in the air like a crazed
person conducting an orchestra. The entire lab was congregated
at the foot of their bay, watching the scene as if it were something
from a movie, a good portion of the postdocs with barely sup-
pressed smiles spilling from their faces. Except for Steven, who
stood at the periphery of the circle, his arms on his chest, staring
somberly at the floor.

"Your genes," Justin kept saying. "I want to see your genes."

From the door I watched Aeden drag his filing cabinet drawer
open and extract the printouts I'd examined. He sat with a hand
held across his mouth while Justin flipped through a mound of
stapled pages, his eyes darting uncomprehendingly from one
sheet to another, no doubt seeing only randomness in the molecular language. He went through the same motions with the other
printouts, and flung the stack on Aeden's desk. It landed with a
thump, like a bird without wings. "You mean to tell me these are
the genes you knocked out?"

Aeden looked at him. "Don't pretend you've never seen them.
You've seen them, Justin. You even said they were promising."

"No, I didn't. I would never say such a thing. Not without a
stitch of evidence. It would be unprofessional of me."

"Unprofessional," Aeden said, with a conspiratorial look at Allegra. But her face was turned to the window.

"Don't patronize me, Aeden," Justin shouted. "I just got off the phone with Carol Levine. She says the gene Craig isolated from his mutant flies has a small internal sequence in its coding region that is unique. She didn't say what it was, of course. But I can tell you this, without knowing anything about it, I can tell you I highly doubt that the sequence is in any of your genes. In fact, I bet you it isn't. I should never have allowed you to knock them out. Clearly they're not what we're looking for."

"This isn't happening." It was Allegra, speaking to the linoleum at her feet.

"You don't know that, Justin," Aeden said. "You don't even know that this Carol person is telling you the truth."

Justin glared at him. "Show me the results."

Aeden shut his eyes.

"C'mon, I want to see those mouse heads of yours. Don't think that because I wear a suit to work I've forgotten how long it takes to analyze a few brains. Not that long, Aeden. It doesn't take a genius to figure out that your results are negative. After three years and two national grant awards, we're going to be scooped by another lab." He glanced behind him, casting a searching eye at the faces gathered around him before looking back away. "Stupid me, trusting your knowledge and intuition as scientists instead of taking matters into my own hands."

"You forget this is our first strain of mice," Aeden said in their defense. "We have two other knockout strains, one for each gene, remember?"

"It doesn't matter," Justin snapped. "If I remember correctly, the three genes you knocked out are very similar to one another."

"That doesn't mean they're doing the same thing. One of them could still have a role in axon guidance."

Justin gave him an exasperated look. "Don't you get it?" he said. "You knocked out the wrong genes." He looked behind him again, this time past the congregation, and spotted me by the door, where I'd remained standing. He grabbed the printouts from Aeden's desk and began to make his way toward me.

Aeden flashed out of his chair, following Justin through the parting mob of postdocs and students. "Where are you going with our sequences, Justin?"

"Where does it look like I'm going?"

"You have no right."

"I have all the right in the world. I'm the head of this lab."

Before I could fully digest what was happening, Justin was standing in front of me. "Take a look at them, Emily. Let me know what you think." He plopped the pages into my arms. Mechanically I curled my fingers around them, astonished at their meager weight, at the springy pliability of paper that seemed to mirror the state of my mind, adrift in shame and confusion. "How long will it take you to examine them?" Justin demanded.

I didn't dare look at Aeden. "A couple of hours."

"How long to find a suitable gene candidate?"

"I don't know," I answered. "I can't predict that."

"But you will find it," Justin said. "In our database."

"I will try."

"Welcome to the project, Emily." A false smile was budding from the corners of Justin's mouth. He held his hand out to me, but thankfully I had no hands to take it.

Everyone in the lab was gathered around us, including Aeden, standing next to Justin. When I finally summoned the courage to look at him, I was bewildered. I had expected to see anger in his face, but there was no anger. He was visibly upset about the situation, but beyond that, there was a shade of disillusionment in his eyes, as if I were a rare butterfly his hopes had been set on, whose damaged wing he'd failed to see; and for a reason I could not begin to put my finger on, it troubled me more than I could say.

"I'll do my best," I said to Justin, and fled to my corner of the lab, to be alone.

PART TWO

A BRIDGE

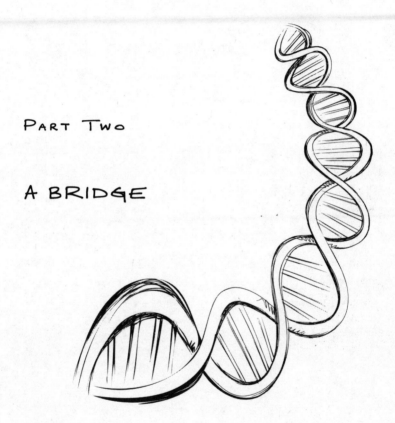

TWELVE YEARS AGO, THE PERIOD IN THE LAB I'M recalling, the belief that there existed a yet-to-be-discovered group of guidance proteins exclusive to the sense of smell was at best an educated guess. There was no evidence to indicate that the molecules that shaped the map of smell during development were any different from the well-known fraternity of axon guidance proteins that accounted for much of the wiring in the brain. In fact, several of these proteins were known to help olfactory axons navigate the bulb. Yet given the thousands of targets olfactory nerve endings need to reach in the bulb to form the map of smell, it was possible, theoretically, that a completely new group of genes existed.

Among the things I had told Justin at the conference in Chicago, something I could distinctly remember saying was that these genes, if they existed, were likely to have sequences unobserved in other genes. They were likely to be related to other axon guidance molecules, I told him, but only insofar as a star is an incandescent mass of gas, or a person is a member of the human race. "They will be the oddballs of their community," I said. Standing with Justin at the refreshments table that day, I'd felt confident enough to speak my mind, sensing as I did that if anyone would hear me out on my crazy theory it was him: a man who seemed to me to be about as guarded around other people as I was.

"And what are these proteins doing, in your opinion?" Justin asked me, clearing his throat from the coffee that tasted like fish piss.

"Directing traffic," I said.

"How?"

A crude example, but the best one I could think of, was a moving walkway in an airport. "Imagine thousands of people in an airport terminal," I said, "all of them needing to reach different gates. Now imagine a series of walkways designated to channel them to their respective gates. The people are the axons, the gates are their targets in the bulb, and the walkways are the proteins. It doesn't need to be a huge group of proteins. It can be a small group, so long as its members can recognize and interact with different types of axons."

Suddenly I'd lost him. He was eyeing a man staring at a conference leaflet near our end of the table—a lab head, according to his name tag.

"Anyway," I said, speaking to Justin's profile. "I hope I've gotten my theory across."

"An unlikely theory," Justin said, loudly enough for the man to hear.

I knew then that *unlikely* meant feasible. The bell call sounded and Justin walked off, and that was the last time I'd spoken to anyone about my theory.

AFTER FLEEING TO MY CORNER OF THE LAB THAT MORNING I wanted to approach Aeden, wanted to explain why Justin had gotten so worked up about the internal sequence in Craig's gene and why it was important. That was the reason I gave myself at the time for wanting to speak to him—the one I was aware of, at least, or willing to admit to myself.

But to approach Aeden after what happened that day, to even get him to talk to me, was harder than I'd anticipated.

In the crowded elevator one morning, on our way up to the lab, Aeden made a point of fixing his eyes on the button panel. When the elevator stopped on our floor he bolted out ahead of me.

"Aeden," I called.

He kept walking. "What do you want?"

The weather was colder, and he was wearing a long black woolen coat I'd never seen on him, reaching almost down to his knees. From behind, it gave him the mysterious air of a magician. "Do you have a moment?" I followed him through the double doors of the lab, into the hallway. "I'd like to talk to you."

"I have mice to dissect," he said, not turning his head to look at me.

He was walking fast, and the gap between us widening. "What about later today?"

"Probably not."

At lunch I went to the cafeteria to look for him, but he wasn't there. I knew he snuck out of the lab during the day to smoke. I'd smelled the cigarettes on him and knew that wherever it was that he went to, it couldn't be far. I searched the campus grounds for about an hour in the hopes of finding the secluded spot where he might be, but it was in vain. When I returned to the lab he was settled in the conference room with his container of food, chatting with Allegra.

In the evening I left the lab shortly after he did and followed him down the street, to the dorm building where most of the postdocs in the lab lived. I wanted to catch up with him but he was talking on his phone, and the intimate tone of his voice told me it wasn't a good idea to interrupt him.

The following morning, and for many days, I scanned the crowded lobby of the building, hoping to see Aeden on his way to the lab. But I never ran into him in the lobby, or in the street.

A few weeks later, late on a Friday afternoon, I saw him descending the stairs of the lecture hall, scanning the packed rows and crowded aisles for a place to sit. Catching his eye, I pointed to the empty seat next to mine, then watched him move right past me, only to settle a few rows farther down, between two perfect strangers.

For the next fifty minutes I sat alone in my seat, unable to make sense of the images being projected on the screen, unable to concentrate on what the renowned stem-cell biologist from Kobe, Japan, whose papers I'd read with fascination, was saying about rewriting a human cell's destiny.

When the lecture ended I left my seat and went to stand outside, in the cool autumn air. I knew that I should give up and leave, but something kept me there, waiting for the Q&A session to end. At last a flourish of clapping came drifting through the open doors, followed by the hubbub of people rising from their chairs. I was standing to one side of the doors, eyeing the multitude of faces flocking up the stairs, when Aeden came charging past me in his black coat, a pack of Parliaments in his hand.

"Aeden?" I said.

"We meet again," he said, and veered north, in the opposite direction from the lab.

"I hate to bother you."

"Then don't."

I trailed behind him anyway, across a lawn of leaves, wanting to catch up with him and not daring to. It was six o'clock in the evening. The light of day was starting to fade, and the air was cold and still and silent but for the distant sounds of York Avenue traffic and the crunching of the leaves under our feet. "We need to talk," I said.

Aeden didn't answer.

Beyond the lawn, behind the Human Resources building, there was a courtyard I'd never seen. Wooden benches with peeling paint stood against three tall walls, facing a sapling growing in a circle of bricks. Aeden went to stand by the tree. He took an orange lighter from his coat pocket and lit a cigarette. I realized this was his hiding place, the place he came to smoke, and to be alone. I felt I shouldn't be there, impinging on his privacy, but I couldn't help myself.

"What is it you want to talk about?" he asked in a resigned voice.

I walked through the gate and went to stand next to him, under the tree. "Why are you evading me?"

He shook his head at me. "Do I need to answer that question, Emily? It's obvious you've been waiting for your chance to jump in, and Justin has been encouraging you all along. 'Welcome to the project.' Did he really expect me to fall for that nonsense? Did *you*?"

"I never agreed to switch projects, Aeden."

He let out a stream of smoke through his nostrils, nodding at the bleached sky above our heads. "That's true. I just assumed you would."

"I should have been honest with you," I said. "As honest and straightforward as you've been with me."

"Is that why you're here?"

"What?" I asked, momentarily thrown off by the question. "No. I want to talk about the sequence, the one the San Diego lab found in their gene. I don't have a clear idea of what it is, but I know for a fact it's not in any of your genes."

"I think that topic was already amply covered. Don't you?" Aeden took another drag from his cigarette. "Look, I don't mean to be rude, but the last thing I want is to discuss my genes with you. If anything I'd like to chill a bit before imaging my next round of enlightening bulbs."

"You're asking me to leave?" I said, though it was clear enough.

"Requesting kindly," Aeden said, releasing an ashen blanket of smoke through his mouth.

I wanted to ask him if he knew how many smokers were diagnosed with lung cancer each year, and of those how many died; the odds weren't in his favor. Instead I found myself saying, "I'm not here because of your genes, Aeden. I'm here because I didn't want you to see me in a bad light after what happened, but it looks like you'll go on seeing me that way no matter what I do or say."

I turned around and began to walk away. I hadn't yet reached the small crooked gate at the end of the courtyard when Aeden called behind me, "Emily, wait."

His next words made me stop. "What brought you to the project?"

CHAPTER 9

O N OUR WAY TO THE TRAMWAY—A NEIGHBOR-
hood diner with pink neon lights tucked like
an oyster in a shell under the Queensboro Bridge—Aeden told me
about Craig Wallace, the star senior postdoc in Justin's lab two
years earlier.

Justin had demoted him for falling behind schedule with his
mice and losing to a competing lab. The next day Craig had gone
into one of the mouse colony rooms of the lab in the Animal Facility and swapped the labels on the cages, making hundreds of
nearly identical brown mice bearing different mutations indis-
tinguishable from one another.

"It took David close to a year to regenotype the mice and
straighten out the mess," Aeden said, dodging a pizza delivery
boy on a bicycle.

"And Craig definitely did it?" I asked.

Aeden looked straight into my eyes. "There's no proof that he
did. By the time the mess was discovered Craig was gone. But who
else could have done it?"

"I'm surprised Justin didn't press charges."

Aeden held a hand to his ear, as if he'd failed to hear me.

"Press charges? Justin wouldn't press charges against a serial killer. An investigation would spoil his precious reputation, not to mention the lab's."

I wanted to laugh about the serial killer part but was fighting off a jabbing headache similar to the one I'd experienced after breaking into Aeden's filing cabinet.

In the diner a Coldplay song I knew Aeden liked was streaming through a loudspeaker on the wall. Snippets of the melody had escaped the earbuds he wore in the lab at night, and I'd grown to like the song myself. It was a sad sort of song, and the place, with its yellow lighting and large empty booths, had the lonely feel of an Edward Hopper painting. But I couldn't have felt less alone.

"What are you having?" Aeden asked, flipping the plastic pages of his menu.

"I'm actually not that hungry." The headache had begun to fade, but I was still feeling too anxious for food.

An elderly woman was sitting all alone across from our booth. There was a stain on her bread, she kept telling the waiter, a red stain she was certain was beet juice. The waiter agreed that the bread was stained—though it wasn't—and when he walked off with the basket of bread I was able to see the woman clearly. She was wearing white elbow-length gloves with a white dress and hat; her shoes were also white, and on her plate was an egg-white omelet and a scoop of cottage cheese. Aeden was observing her too, and when our eyes met we smiled at each other, mutually intrigued.

"So why smell research?" he asked me.

The answer I gave him came out so effortlessly I might have been preparing it in my head all along. "I was allergic to grass growing up, especially cut grass." I gazed out the window, noticing the street outside, glowing with the lights of the bridge towering over us. What I told him next was unexpected. "I spent most of my childhood indoors, alone, never playing with anyone. My father was always worried about me. It bothered him that I had no friends. Even in my teens, after I outgrew my allergy, I kept looking for excuses to stay at home, or in his lab. He ran a small chemistry lab at the medical school in Rockford. Anyway, summer weekends he had to practically drag me out of the house to the local mall, Lino's for pizza, sometimes even the Navy Pier in Chicago, the beach in Evanston, wherever he thought I might run into people my own age, which I did, of course, but it was pointless. I'm not a very sociable person."

"I think I've deduced that much about you," Aeden said, smiling across the table at me.

The waiter had brought our orders: blackout cake for Aeden and lemon meringue pie for me, plus coffees. I sank my fork into the pie, savoring the sweet lemon tang.

"Do you think it shaped your life?" he asked.

"What do you mean?"

"Your sensitivity to the smell of cut grass, would you say that it has affected who you are?"

"I don't know. What you're asking me in a way is what came first, the chicken or the egg. The answer I've been divulging now for several years is that the egg came first. A mutant egg."

"Funny," Aeden said with a frown, clearly finding as much humor in the joke as my last date had. I thought he would leave it at that, but then he said, "I don't think it's just you, Emily. I think we all feel like mutants in our own way."

Hearing him say that, I felt a weight inside of me had been lifted. "You're probably right, Aeden. The problem is I don't know what everyone else is feeling. I'm not inside anyone else to know. But how about you? What brought you to the project?"

<hr>

IT WASN'T UNTIL LATER THAT NIGHT, UNTIL AFTER WE LEFT THE Tramway and reached the scaffolding of our dorm and had been standing out in the chilly night air for a while, discussing the pros and cons of smell hypersensitivity, that Aeden told me about his mother.

The accident had happened over a Christmas holiday during which he'd accompanied her on a last-minute shopping errand and was following her down a flight of stairs, to the underground lot where they'd parked the car. His mother slipped and fell down the stairs, landing on the concrete floor.

"When I first saw her going down I thought one of her earrings had come loose and she was bending down to look for it. The fall was so slow, so unreal. The next thing I know, my mother's lying motionless at the bottom of the stairs." He flicked ashes from his cigarette on the pavement. "A week later she began to complain. Food was flavorless and she couldn't smell anything, not even a burning pot. A month later they told her the impact had sheared off the nerve endings in her olfactory bulb, and she was diagnosed with anosmia. That was four years ago. The latest prognosis from the specialist in New Jersey is that she will never recover her sense of smell. The worst part of it is that my mother essentially lived to smell the roses. She loved gardening and cooking. Especially cooking. There was always a cake baking in the oven, and she would throw dinner parties every weekend. It was her thing to have people over. These days it's a good day if she can get out of bed. I'm lucky if I can get her on the phone."

Aeden dragged on his cigarette and let out a soft stream of smoke. I noticed that his nose had a slightly veered septum, and found myself drawn to the imperfection.

"So I figured," he said, "if I could contribute to our understanding of how the map of smell is formed, someone in the future might be able to restore a severed bulb. Not that my mother will live to see the benefits. The kind of cure I'm talking about is decades away, and my mother is in her sixties."

"Do you blame yourself for the accident?" I asked.

Aeden shrugged. "My hands were caught up with shopping bags and my mother was wearing high heels. So no, I don't blame myself. But if I could turn back the clock, if I could go back in time, I would have let go of those bags much sooner than I did."

Level with his voice I could hear the seashore drift of vehicles on the FDR Drive that lulled me to sleep at night, and make out their lights. Aeden was on his last cigarette and I almost didn't want him to finish it, knowing that our conversation would come to an end.

He fixed his eyes on mine again. "I don't know if what you're looking to find is out there, Emily. I don't even know that it exists. But if it does, I doubt you'll find it in the database. It's pretty incomplete. David built it in his spare time. I don't know that he even knew what he was doing. Many genes are missing from his database. I know this for a fact. If I were you I wouldn't set my hopes too high." He tossed the burning butt of his cigarette and turned toward the sidewalk.

"You're leaving?" I asked, catching the inflection of my voice. It was unrealistic of me to expect anything from him, to be disappointed.

"I need to photograph some bulbs and prepare for tomorrow."

"What's happening tomorrow?"

"Our second line of knockout mice. We're hoping to see something interesting." Aeden looked away from me, at the empty avenue. I wondered if he could read the doubt I was feeling in my face. "It's getting late. I better run."

"Good night," I said.

"Good night, Emily," he said, and hurried off. I watched him head across the street toward the campus, with his coat flapping open behind him like a pair of wings. There was an awkwardness in his stride I found touching, something about it that brought my father to mind, except my father's way of walking was not brisk but slow, very slow: his right leg always dragging a beat behind his left, as if he were moving along a path too dangerous and unknown to advance properly upon with any freedom.

"Good luck with your experiment," I suddenly shouted, the words just slipping out of my mouth. But Aeden was a long way ahead, and he gave no indication of hearing me. In a way, I hoped he hadn't. To wish him luck was a mistake, because I hadn't really meant it, and because at the end of the day science has nothing to do with luck, but with truth, and the truth does not always make one happy.

CHAPTER 10

DURING HIS YEARS AS A CHEMIST, AND FOR MOST of his life, my father aimed to resolve the structure of a sodium/proton exchanger: a revolving-door type of protein that sweeps sodium and hydrogen ions in and out of living cells, and without which many life forms on earth would not exist.

My father devised a way to extract the membrane-bound protein from bacterial cells and reconstitute it to a purified liquid suspension so clear and inodorous it could have passed for water. The goal was then to find the conditions that would drive the protein molecules to form a crystal lattice from which the position of its atoms could be deduced, the three-dimensional structure of the protein resolved, and the inner workings of the revolving door gleaned. But the molecules, by their very nature, were disinclined to mingle, much less form a crystal lattice pure enough to diffract a high-powered X-ray beam neatly on a film.

It wasn't until much later in his career, when I was in my late teens, that my father came to produce high-quality crystals in his lab, on a rainy autumn day.

The night he succeeded, it was dark outside and he hadn't returned home. No one was answering the phone in the lab and when I tried him in the office the line went straight to voicemail: *This is Roger Apell. I'm sorry I'm not here to take your call, but if you leave your name and number and a detailed message telling me what this is about I will get back to you.* To make matters worse, two of my classmates from school were in our den, waiting with headphones for him to arrive: my father offered tutoring on the side.

The phone in the kitchen started ringing, and it was my father. "Come over," he said.

"To the lab?" I asked.

"I want you to see something."

"It's pelting rain outside."

"Call a limo."

"A limo?"

"Don't ask questions, Emily. Just come over."

There were no limousines in Rockford that I knew of, only a modest car service company whose survival hinged on nearby Chicago and the O'Hare Airport.

"You're sure you want me to go there, Dad?"

"You heard me."

After getting rid of the two boys in our den, telling them my father was stuck in his lab with an important breakthrough in the hopes that this might actually turn out to be true, I rode my bicycle three miles west along the narrow shoulder of the road, vehicles honking and flashing their headlights at me, to the College of Medicine.

In the lobby of my father's building I made out singing, and as I approached the lab—two rooms at the end of a sinewy ground floor untouched in decades but for a recently erected DNA sequencing center—I smelled beer in the air. A homegrown student whose eyes were often troublingly red was sitting cross-legged on a bench, shoulder to shoulder with Pavel, the head technician of the lab for as long as I could remember. Pavel was a colossal man with colossal hands, whose lethargic way of carrying himself around the lab made him always seem to be either drunk or afflicted with some tender and agonizing pain smack in the center of his heart. But that night he was buoyant with happiness, singing "Dark Eyes" in Russian at the top of his lungs. "Hey, you," he said, summoning me with his empty beer bottle. "Come join us."

I charged past him in my dripping raincoat.

"What's the matter, Emily, you don't like 'Ochi Chernye'?"

"You know I do." I actually did, very much, ever since he'd played the song on his viola over a Thanksgiving dinner at our house.

"So live a little. Results are fantastic."

But *fantastic* had the slippery feel of one of those sinkholes people were always disappearing into in Florida. One false move and you were done for. "We'll sing and cry together later, Pavel," I said. In retrospect, nothing could have been more true.

I found my father in his office, head bent into the stereomicroscope on his desk. The beehive-like dishes were piled so high all I could see of him was a tuft of white hair. "You won't believe this," he said, raising his face from the eyepiece.

"Perfect crystals," I said skeptically. It wasn't my first time there at that hour of night, his first time calling me with a false alarm.

My father stood up. "Take a look." He gestured with his hand toward the dish on the stage, perched under a yellow spill of light as familiar to me as the lighting in our kitchen.

I lowered myself into his chair and looked through the eyepiece. I had seen crystals before: needles with bright cutting edges and polygons and cylinders and cigar-shaped rods that looked like the real thing and disintegrated at the slightest nudge of a pipette tip, dissolving back into the medium in which they'd been born. But these were different.

I turned the focus knob back and forth between my fingers, like my father had taught me, and saw hundreds of cubes suspended brightly in the medium, reflecting the yellow scope light like grains of sand on a sunny shore. There was a toughness about them, a finality of purpose the other crystals had never had, and I imagined my father's protein packed tightly, invisibly inside each one: thousands of revolving doors locked hand in hand by unseen interactions extending in six different planes. If they held their own against the X-ray beam it would be unprecedented, a biochemical feat equivalent to putting a man on the moon.

I looked up at him, trying to contain my enthusiasm. "What happens next?"

My father was standing with his back to the torrent of sleet falling steadily across the window. In his world of sacrifice and unfailing optimism it was as though everything had already happened: the crystals transported to his collaborators in Chicago, the 3-D structure of the protein resolved, long-overdue papers published back-to-back, the lab expanded and renewed. His future secured, as well as mine.

"Nothing much," he said. "This is it, Emily."

"It's not," I said. "You know it isn't. We're not done yet."

"Of course we are," my father said. "This is the moment."

But in fact everything ended there.

A few days later, despite their promising appearance, the

crystals produced a diffraction pattern too weak to be accurately interpreted. Something in their internal arrangement was off, and they did not hold up against the X-ray beam. And while my father painstakingly worked around the clock to try to solve the problem, playing around with temperature and tweaking the acidity of the buffer in the hopes of growing better crystals, a crystallography lab in Germany we'd never heard of came out with a paper in *Nature* explaining in full detail the revolving-door mechanism.

Two years after that my father's lab was shut down for lack of funding, and my father found himself a retiree at age sixty-five. The day he died I got a call in Champaign with an urgent message. I hurried out of the calculus class I'd enrolled in, to the admissions office, and picked up the phone: black, antiquated, medieval-looking. A nurse was on the other end of the line, calling from Rockford Memorial Hospital. My father had suffered a stroke and wanted to see me.

When I arrived he was lying on a cot with a needle sticking out of his forearm, hooked to a feeding machine through a thin plastic tube. The right side of his face was paralyzed. When he spoke it was from one corner of his mouth, the words sounding like mindless blabber. The surgeon, before stepping quietly out of the room and leaving me alone with my father, told me there was a blood-filled bulge in the left hemisphere of his brain, so deep it was basically inoperable.

The room had a single window, tall and netted, that showed the limpid spring day outside, the cold sun high in the sky. I took my father's hand and held it, and heard him tell me he'd been a failure. That he had failed me in every way. I told him he hadn't. I told him he had no control over what other people were doing across the Atlantic, and about me, as far as I was concerned, it wasn't his fault, how I was. It was just who I was, how I'd been born. There was fear in his eyes, watching me speak, fear in his eyes when I tried to let go of his hand. That's when I told him everything would be okay. I was a big girl now, I could take care of myself, I would be fine. He didn't believe me, but after a while he fell asleep, and never woke up again.

The last year of his life he drove to his lab every morning, out of habit, and home again, stopping on his way back at the public library and staying there for hours. After his death I imagined my father sitting in that library with his coffee thermos, a legal pad and pen, and swollen notebooks decades old, going over the chemical recipes with which he'd reared crystals like sugar cubes, trying in vain to figure out where he went wrong.

———

SO I WAS WORRIED ABOUT AEDEN. IN PARTICULAR, I WAS WORRIED about his unrelenting faith in his three genes, and his apparent blindness to all the evidence mounting against them.

After analyzing their third line of mice, Aeden and Allegra failed to show up at a group meeting where they were scheduled to present images of their bulbs. It was apparent to everyone at the table that they had nothing to show but negative results: mouse brains with unaltered maps of smell. Yet cages with live mice inside them continued to appear every day on Aeden's bench, and at the end of each day he and Allegra would sit for hours in their bay, studying the brain images on his laptop.

From my desk the images were impossible to see, and the language in which the two spoke to each other, in lowered voices, was so technical and foreign to me that for all my reading and rereading the papers in the field, I was unable to form a clear picture in my head. And yet despite this I knew full well that whatever they were seeing was not what they wanted, or had expected, to see—not what Aeden had had in mind to find when he'd come to the lab three years earlier, after his mother's accident.

Late in the evenings, after everyone was gone for the day and it was just the two of us in the room, I would sometimes hear him talking on the phone with his mother, inquiring how her day had gone: "Did Dad get the tree?" After a brief pause: "Who's decorating it this year?" A burst of fresh laughter across my desk wall. "Mark?"

Other nights, when he wasn't on the phone with his mother, or discussing the injustices of global politics with the lady who mopped the floors, or humming along with his iPod, Aeden would sit silently in front of the mouse bulb on his screen, as though he were racking his brain trying to understand what had led to the unwanted image, and where he had gone wrong.

At times like these I fantasized about turning the clock back so that he might start over again, on the right foot. At times like these I also found myself rehashing our Tramway Diner evening, cutting across the moments and rearranging them into long shimmering sequences, different from the original, and yet the picture always the same: his smile across the table, the feel of his hand on my elbow crossing the street, and beneath the scaffolding of our dorm building his gray eyes fixed on mine. *I don't know if what you're looking to find is out there. I don't even know that it exists.*

CHAPTER 11

S INCE THAT EVENING SIX WEEKS HAD PASSED. OC-
tober had merged with November, and a lonely
Thanksgiving dinner in my dorm had given way to snow-layered
sidewalks and men with woolen caps rolled down to their eyes
selling trees in the street, cajoling me into a false state of merri-
ment. Christmas party invites were posted in every elevator on
campus, and then the parties had already taken place and everyone in the lab was gone. Except for a graduate student coming in
the mornings to work on her thesis, and David dropping by every
so often to sort through shipments of perishables and check on
the mice in the facility, I was practically alone in the lab.

The doors at the end of the hallway would slam into each
other with a backlog of air and I'd jump in my chair, only to hear
the tick of the clock on the wall and the rasp of my laptop fan,
and that all-engorging silence between Aeden's desk and mine,
throughout the empty bays of the lab.

For all that I enjoyed having nothing to distract me, it was
sometimes depressing. Especially at night, with the bridge illuminated like a Christmas tree outside my window. To add to
my discontent, the lab's database had come full circle in a dis-

appointing way. Aeden and Allegra's three genes weren't in it, which meant that other genes expressed in the bulb—possibly those I was looking to find—could be missing as well, though I didn't know this for certain.

Among the few unknown genes that I had found, there was only one that gave me hope. I had aligned its sequence against several axon guidance genes, including Aeden and Allegra's, and found a few hazy similarities. On the other hand, the difference, defined by a small segment in my gene of letters repeating at almost timed intervals, stood out like a tidal wave in an ocean. I didn't know if this had anything to do with what I was looking to find, or what the San Diego lab claimed to be seeing in the mutant fly gene. But it did seem special, or at least different from anything I'd ever seen.

———

IT WAS DURING THE LAST WEEK OF THAT DECEMBER, WHILE EVeryone was away, that Justin showed up again in the lab.

He'd been away for two months, at conferences and seminars. That is what he'd informed everyone in his mass emails, and also what the asides in his private messages to me, inquiring about my progress in the project, had hinted at: *sick of hotel food, left my comfy sheep slippers behind, I sometimes wish I had a companion to travel with*.

But his face, when he showed up in my bay, was lobster sunburned, and his jacket sportive and casual compared to the stiff suits he usually wore, and when in the back seat of a yellow cab on our way to lunch I pressed him about his whereabouts, he told me he'd been in Florida.

"Doing what?"

"Flying."

"A plane?"

"I should think so. I haven't flown a kite since I was twelve."

"You never told me you could fly a plane."

I was actually amazed, not because I doubted he had the cool-headedness to pilot an aircraft, but because I somehow couldn't imagine him liking being up in the air. Justin smiled nonchalantly at me, and moving closer to my side of the seat, settled his right hand on my kneecap. I thought of asking him what he was doing, but his touch was so light and unassuming it almost felt as if he were holding on to me for balance more than for anything else.

At the restaurant, a place on Broadway with padded red leather walls and dim illumination whose name I've forgotten, Justin ordered two onion soups for starters, and for our main course steak frites, accompanied by two glasses of a Napa cabernet. When the soups arrived he made a neat little bib of his napkin and began to eat without me, while eyeing a woman sitting alone at a table nearby. I wanted to talk to him about the sequence fragment, but for the next half hour or so, while he ate and eyed the woman, it was mainly Justin who did the talking.

He'd purchased a small aircraft, a two-seat Piper, against his parents' wishes, and so they knew nothing about it. But it had been a lifelong dream of his to own a plane by age forty, and if not now, when? It was difficult enough to figure out how to be happy.

"Does it make you happy to fly a plane?" I asked.

"Immensely."

"How come?"

"I can forget who I am. Up there it's just me and the plane, and nobody else. I feel more alive than I do down here. Even my skin smells different."

"That's because you probably can't smell it at high altitude."
Justin laughed.

I didn't want to ask him what it was about himself that he wanted to forget. I didn't want to get into a personal conversation with him.

"At any rate, my parents will be finding out very shortly because I'm flying my Piper to Maine in just a few hours. It's where we converge, you know, every Christmas, my mother and father and my three sisters with their husbands and their brats. For a week we all live like family, in a very large and very beautiful house with a full-blown view of the sea. You've never seen anything like it, Emily. It's like living inside a ship. Here, I'll show you a picture."

He raised his BlackBerry from the table and scrolled the screen for a picture but luckily found none to show me. "Pity, I thought I'd photographed the house." He laid the BlackBerry down.

"Can we talk about the finding, Justin?"

"That's right, your gene. What about it?" He picked up his second glass of wine.

"There's something I'm still trying to figure out. A pattern. I don't know that it has anything to do with what Craig found, but it looks special, different. I can't explain how."

"What you need is a vacation."

"I'm having one now," I said. "As we speak." Though I didn't consider having lunch with Justin a vacation, I was grateful for the meal, and for the company. "This is actually my first time out of the campus neighborhood in weeks."

"Precisely my point. You shouldn't be spending your holiday cooped up in the lab. You should be out and about, enjoying yourself. I have an idea."

I was worried he was about to suggest I go with him to Maine, but he didn't. He produced a wallet from the inside of his jacket, took out a wad of vouchers, and laid them on the table: Carnegie Hall, the Museum of Modern Art, the Metropolitan Museum of Art, the Frick Collection, Body Worlds, a singles' night out in the Empire State Building observatory, a Broadway show called *Wicked,* another one called *Rent.*

"You don't want them?" I asked.

"They're all yours."

"Are you sure?"

"Positive."

"That's very kind of you, Justin." I gathered the vouchers and warily dropped the wad into my handbag. I could already see them collecting dust in my night table drawer, could easily see myself throwing them down the garbage chute outside my dorm room in a month, maybe two. I had little to no interest in spending time outside the lab, much less at a singles' night out. The likelihood of finding someone suitable for me at that type of event was so remote I would have been better off placing an ad in *Psychology Today:* "Girl seeks intimacy."

"How old are you?" Justin asked me.

I looked at him. "Twenty-eight," I said, though I was closer to twenty-nine. "Why do you ask?"

"I see you and I see myself twelve, fifteen years ago. So single-minded and ambitious, so alone."

I smiled at him. "You mean you're not like that anymore?"

"Are you happy, Emily?"

"Happy." I wondered if he seriously expected me to answer the question. Then I took the safe route. "How do you define happiness?"

"Are you satisfied with your present life, your personal circumstances?"

The way he was looking at me, with his eyes warily centered on mine, made me feel as though whatever answer I gave him would be more about him than it would be about me.

"I can't imagine any other way of life," I finally said, guessing this would please him.

"That's what I thought."

"Did you?" I asked, but I wasn't surprised.

"Yes," Justin said, with a satisfied face. "I just wanted confirmation."

I lifted my coat from the empty chair beside me and wrapped my arms around it, feeling uncomfortably cold.

"You're cold?" he asked me, fanning himself with his dessert menu.

"Yes," I said, suddenly annoyed. "It's cold in here, Justin."

Justin chuckled. "It must be eighty degrees in here, Emily."

CHAPTER 12

WHAT STANDS OUT IN MY MEMORY OF THAT December, aside from what Justin said to me in the restaurant, is stumbling a few days later upon the Metropolitan Museum of Art.

I had spent the entire morning in the lab, submitting the segment of my gene with the repeating letters to pattern-recognition programs in the hopes of pinning down a motif. After several hours the search had produced no results, and left me staring at the ATGCs filling the small window on my screen with the same incomprehension. Yet something about the way the letters repeated was familiar.

I was dizzy from looking at the screen, and across the street the metal hamper in my bathroom was threatening to pop open with dirty clothes. It was a Sunday. Sunday was the day I vacuumed my dorm and shopped for food and did the laundry, and I hadn't done any of these things in more than two weeks. A shopping list was in my coat pocket, but the minute I stepped out of the lab and felt the fresh air on my face, and saw the avenue bathed in sunlight, I trailed off, in a different direction.

Instead of heading to Gristedes, the neighborhood supermarket, I headed west, toward the place where I'd left Allegra's hairclip lying on the counter. The next thing I knew, the campus neighborhood was far behind me, and I was gazing at Christmas trees lying discarded on sidewalks and couples with strollers and Starbucks shops wafting the smell of coffee into the cold sunny street. The day was blindingly bright, and the ATGC letters swam in my mind. Something about their pattern was missing from my frame of reference, something I was blind to, like a person with anosmia is blind to smell.

I ventured past the Nectar diner, toward Fifth Avenue, and caught sight of a building that seemed to span the entire length of the block. Tourist buses and food carts were parked at the foot of wide steps ascending to an arched entryway where there was a giant placard with a consonant-riddled name I could hardly begin to pronounce. From where I stood I could see a long line of people waiting at the entrance of the building. I was tempted to keep walking, but the vouchers Justin had given me were still in my handbag, and before I knew it my feet had taken me across the street, up the crowded steps, to the end of the line.

Inside the museum I wandered the cavernous first floor, navigating my way around glass-encased jewelry and pottery and drinking cups from the Roman Empire. I rented an audio guide from the front desk and walked the floor some more, and after a series of long-winded explanations from a British female voice I pulled the plugs out of my ears and found my way to the nearest cafeteria.

At the register I paid for a cold sandwich and a coffee and sat at a small table overlooking Central Park. Beyond the glass I could see white clouds roaming the sky, and beneath them benches flanking a path that wound all the way uphill into the distance.

The symmetry brought the gene back to mind, swooped me right back to that impossible-to-crack pattern. Why couldn't I see it? What was it about it that made me feel I was in two places at the same time?

According to biologist François Jacob, whose biography I'd read, there was something called night science—as opposed to day science. Day science meant using the side of your brain involved in thinking. Night science meant using your intuition. Day science meant looking at the sequence of a gene and seeing nothing in it you could understand. Night science meant looking at it again with a vague presentiment, a hazy sensation not yet consolidated into thought.

I abandoned the sandwich and the coffee and went up a wide staircase with brass handrails to the second floor. A long hall of tall opalescent ceilings led into several rooms without doors. I entered one of the rooms and gazed at the paintings on the walls. Some of them left me cold, despite the swarms of people surrounding them and the angry pleas of the guard to step back, while other, apparently less well-known works struck me as spectacular: a pregnant woman cradling a cat on her lap, snow-coated trees at the edge of a crystal-blue lake.

I drifted across one room, into another, past a painting of naked women dancing in a circle, into another room, past the portrait of a woman with a mustache, into yet another room, smaller than the rest. It was inside this small room, possibly the quietest on that floor, that I first saw him, studying me undisturbed from a wall. He sat with his elbows resting on a desk cluttered with folders and books, gazing at me with eyes so intensely troubled it was as though he'd suffered some bottomless loss from which there was no conceivable recovery. I walked slowly over to him until I was standing practically inches away from his face, imagining the smell of turpentine.

His resemblance to Aeden was uncanny: the same gray eyes and acute gaze, the same thick eyebrows jutting into the bridge of an aquiline nose, dark hair tossed back from his wide forehead. If not for the beard and the priestly looking shirt the man was wearing, and for the fact that the painting was obviously old and hanging in a museum, I would have thought he was Aeden.

"Repin. My favorite artist in the room."

I turned away from the painting. Behind me was a man about my age, or slightly older. There was a badge on his shirt that said MET, with his picture on it.

"He reminds me of someone I know," I said in a casual voice.

"I hope your friend has better luck," the man said. "This one threw himself down a stairwell and died when he was thirty-three years old."

"That's a sad story," I said, recalling what Aeden had told me about his mother. I stared back at the canvas, trying to visualize the man with a paintbrush in his hand, and couldn't. His hands were resting on either side of an open book.

"Are you an artist?" the man behind me asked.

"No," I answered in my blandest voice, hoping he would go away.

"Do you paint at all?"

"I wish I knew how," I caught myself saying, and realized it was true.

I turned around and gave the man a closer look: pressed white shirt and corn-blond hair, a straight-shooting face, mainstream and modest. The sort of guy my father would have been delighted to see me with if he'd been alive.

"Did he make other paintings before he died?" I asked, glancing at the portrait.

The man gave me a funny look. "That's Garshin," he said, nodding toward the canvas. "Not Repin. Garshin was a Russian author. He's the one with the tragic life."

This surprised me. I'd been under the impression that we were talking about the same person, that the artist and the model were one and the same. "I thought it was a self-portrait," I said.

"Oh, no. That would have required a mirror right around here." He raised an arm in the air and held it out between us, flashing an image through my head.

"A mirror?" I asked. It was as though someone had miraculously handed me a sheet of paper I'd crumpled long ago, having dismissed its vital contents as unimportant. "I need to leave."

He followed me across the room, to the nearest exit. "There's a self-portrait of van Gogh two rooms down."

I stopped and turned around to look at him. In a city of eight million people, it was unlikely that we would ever cross paths again. "Maybe some other time," I said.

The man smiled at me, a sweet grin displaying the gap between his two front teeth. "John Cavalier," he said.

I shook his hand, chalk-dry and smelling faintly of some organic flammable substance. "Thank you, John," I said, not volunteering my name. "You've been very helpful. More than you will ever know."

A question mark appeared on his face, but before he could put thoughts into words I was gone.

———

THE SKY OUTSIDE HAD FADED INTO EVENING. ON THE SIDEWALK, awnings had vanished and stores were locked up for the day. Apartment windows I hadn't seen before were glowing from the inside, and the few people remaining on the street were walking fast, as if eager to reach wherever they were headed to. It was one of those winter late afternoons when standing on a corner, waiting for the light, one can sometimes get to feeling that some essential and irrecoverable moment has passed. But that wasn't how I felt. What I felt then, rushing through the streets, was that whatever might have passed me by, whatever I'd missed having or experiencing, was nothing compared to what I had discovered.

In the lab a handful of people had returned from their vacations, including Allegra, who was sitting on a bench, blasting a hair dryer at a grid of biological slides. On her lab coat was a yellow smear from the potassium ferrocyanide of the neuron-staining mixture. As I hurried past her she smiled reflexively at me, and I realized that I was smiling at her; that in fact, I had been smiling all along.

On my laptop screen was the sequence I'd been examining before leaving the lab. I had probed the letters for days, attempting to draw a theme from their arrangement and failing miserably, never realizing what that theme could be, or that the solution to seeing it was so simple.

I color-coded the ATGC letters to yellow, red, blue, and green. I bolded the font and shrank the letters to tiny blocks, then minimized them further, until the blocks merged into a line of alternating greens and reds and blues and yellows followed by the same exact colors but in reverse, and then I remember gasping for air. One half of the sequence was the mirror image of the other, like two arms of a bridge.

My father once said to me, shortly before he died, that a discovery is nothing but a moment. The moment when a truth, otherwise obscured, reveals itself, and your eyes are the only pair of eyes in the world to see it, and your mind the only mind to comprehend the truth and certainty of what you see. The moment is all you're left with, because that is all you will ever care to remember. Not the published paper that will end up on a shelf or in a filing cabinet, not the grant, not even the prize (*if you should be so lucky to receive one*), but the moment.

"Aeden," I said, and heard the echo of my voice.

No one was there, not at his desk and not anywhere. I was alone in the lab, and the clock on the wall indicated that several hours had passed since I'd stormed into the main room and charged past Allegra. It also indicated, amazingly enough, that the moment my father had spoken of was already behind me.

CHAPTER 13

F OR WEEKS I WANTED TO APPROACH AEDEN WITH the news, but Justin, wanting me to run more tests on the gene, and also concerned about word getting out and leaking all the way across the country to the San Diego lab, had instructed me not to. The morning Aeden and I were scheduled to confer with Justin in his office, I emailed Aeden an hour before and asked him to meet me on the East River promenade.

When I descended the ramp he was there, slouched by the railing in his long black coat. An icy wind was blowing from lower Manhattan, sweeping his hair away from his face. My plan was to tell him about the finding and Justin's decision regarding it, so that he would be less taken aback when we met later. But when his gaze fell on me I realized that what I wanted, had been craving all along, was to have this one private moment with him, away from the lab.

I waved at him, but he didn't reciprocate. Instead he stared back at the water and raised the cigarette he was holding to his mouth.

I hurried over to where he stood. "Justin made me swear not to say anything until the meeting," I said. "But it didn't feel right not to tell you beforehand. I found a gene candidate, in the database. I don't know that it's related to the gene Craig found, but it looks promising."

Aeden smiled at me with effort, looking mildly intrigued. "Is it what you've been looking to find?" he asked.

"I don't know," I said. "I think it could be."

"You'll need to knock it out."

"That's where you come in. Justin says you're the most qualified person in the lab to do the job. He says if you put your mind to it you could engineer a knockout in just months. We could work together."

Aeden shook his head. "I can't work with you, Emily." He sounded almost indignant. "I'm happy for you, but I have my own experiment."

I nodded, trying to hide my disappointment. "I thought this project was important to you."

"It is. That's why I haven't lost faith in my genes."

I let his words sit for a moment, seeing no loophole around them. Then I said, "I understand how you feel, Aeden. The first time I saw your genes I thought they looked good on paper, but I also had a strong suspicion that they wouldn't turn out to have the role you'd hoped."

"The first time?" Aeden said.

"I came across your sequences before Justin gave them to me," I said quickly, realizing my mistake.

"Where?" Aeden asked. He was suddenly standing to his full height, blocking the view of the bridge.

"The database," I lied.

"David's database?"

"Yes," I said, and it was here that things took a wrong and ir-reversible turn.

Aeden reached into his coat pocket for another cigarette, then changed his mind. "That's impossible," he said.

"Impossible?" I said, feeling dread curdle my stomach.

"About a year ago, when David built his library, Allegra and I wanted to know if our genes were in it. We tried to isolate them. Nothing caught. They're not in his library, so they can't be in the database. There's no way you could have seen them there."

I looked toward the railing, at the river's shifting surface, and back at him. "The truth is, Aeden, I took the printouts from your filing cabinet. It's not the sort of thing I've ever done before, or will ever do again. I'm sorry." I glanced down at my watch, making out the dials through a fog. "It's getting late," I said. "We should start heading to the meeting."

Aeden just stared at me. It was as though I'd suggested he go jump in the river.

"What do I tell Justin?" I asked, when it was clear he wasn't going to respond. I couldn't look at him; I stared at the brick-layered ground between us.

"You can tell him to go fuck himself."

———————

JUSTIN WAS GAZING DREAMILY OUT THE WINDOW OF HIS OFFICE. In a corner of the room an espresso machine was puffing steam. I'd smelled the coffee outside the door, but it was the sight of croissants layered on a silver tray that made my stomach turn as though I might throw up.

After wavering by the door I crossed the room and sank into

the couch in front of him. The printed pages of my gene were on the coffee table, with the bridge motif highlighted.

"You look like you saw a ghost," Justin said from his chair. "Let me fix you a coffee." He uncrossed his legs to stand, but didn't. "What's the problem?"

"Aeden isn't coming," I said, holding back a sudden impulse to shed tears.

"Of course he is."

"He isn't. I just spoke with him. He's not interested. He says he has his own experiment."

"He has no choice but to be interested. When he shows up, let me do the talking."

"He won't show up."

"Yes, he will."

"Maybe someone else in the lab can help me make the mouse, maybe Steven or Eduardo, or Wendy, maybe even David."

Justin shook his head. "Aeden is the most qualified person to do the job."

"Steven is just as experienced."

"And nowhere near as skillful. We'll get scooped waiting for Steven to engineer a mouse." Justin stood up abruptly and walked to the espresso machine. With his back to me, he fixed himself a coffee. "Is there something you want to tell me?" he asked in an insinuating tone.

I was contemplating a full-fledged confession when Karen appeared at the door, looking very proper and dignified in one of her shoulder-padded blouses, her silver hair pulled back neatly from her face. "Do you need anything before I take my break, Justin?"

"Please tell Aeden we're waiting for him."

For ten long minutes I stared at my shoes while Justin drank his coffee. Just as he was finishing his second cup, Aeden walked into the room and sat on the metal folding chair next to Justin, facing me.

"Emily made a breakthrough," Justin said. He pointed at the pages on the table. "It's all there."

Aeden didn't move. I could feel his eyes on me.

Justin raised the page with the motif and held it out to him. To my surprise, Aeden took it. He sat with his head lowered to the page, studying the sequence, and after about a minute handed it back to Justin. "I'll look at the gene more closely later. I'm sure I'll know where to find it, won't I, Emily?"

I met his eyes and knew he wasn't about to mention what I'd done, knew that he was bigger than that.

"Can one of you please tell me what's going on?" Justin demanded.

"Nothing," Aeden said, and smiled at me.

"Then keep it that way. I haven't got all day." Slowly at first, reining in his enthusiasm, and gradually picking up speed, Justin went on to describe my gene, the motif in its sequence and how its mirror symmetry recalled a bridge. What became of the motif in the protein, what it did at a functional level, was anyone's guess. There was no crystallography data to answer the question, and there probably wouldn't be any for a long time. What was important now was to test the function of the gene, and to do so immediately. If it turned out to have a role in shaping the map of smell, and if there were other genes similar to it, we would be in business.

"Imagine the possibilities, Aeden. The long-term applications," Justin said, sweeping the air with a hand for emphasis.

"Congenital smell disorders, acquired smell disorders, the building of an artificial nose, maybe even an artificial brain. But to test the function of the gene we need to engineer a knockout mouse. If something comes out of the work, and I'm sure it will, you will be second author in Emily's paper."

"I wouldn't have it any other way," Aeden said. It took me a moment to realize he was being sarcastic.

"What do you want?" Justin asked him.

"I want nothing from you, Justin. I'm not getting involved in Emily's work." He looked at me here, as if to make sure that I'd understood. "I have my own work to worry about."

In a lowered voice, Justin said, "I think you owe it to the lab to make this mouse, Aeden."

"I don't owe you anything. I've been supported by an individual fellowship from the National Institutes of Health. I still am."

"What about your mice? The thousands of dollars it cost to make them, the hundreds of dollars it's costing the lab to maintain your colony in the facility?"

"If the lab can't afford to finance my work, that's your fault, Justin." Aeden rolled his eyes at the Persian rug under our feet, the walnut bookcase by the door with travel mementos and first editions of seminal books, including a framed drawing by Ramón y Cajal of the branching axons of a Purkinje cell.

Justin ignored the dig. "I'm not sure you realize that at this stage of the game you have no choice but to make this mouse, Aeden."

"What if I refuse?" Aeden asked casually.

"Then I'll have to ask David to sacrifice your mice as soon as this meeting is over. It's a useless colony and you know it."

Aeden stared icily at him. "If David as much as goes near

my mice I'll be out of here today, and you'll never hear from me again."

"You'll do what Craig did?" Justin said, making a worried face.

"Don't fuck with me, Justin. I'm dead serious."

For a while no one spoke. I could hear Karen back at her desk, tapping at her keyboard, and feel the wind outside fighting to get in. Justin was staring pensively out the window. He raised his hand to the glass and rapped it with his knuckles; then, clearing his throat, he turned his attention back to Aeden. "So leave," he said. "You can leave right now if that's what you want."

Aeden's knee gave a little jolt.

"With your publication record of the last three years I'm sure you'll do brilliantly." Justin continued, "What do *you* think? You think he stands a chance of having his own lab?" To my dismay, I realized he was addressing me.

Aeden made a movement to stand up, but he didn't. He remained seated on the metal chair, his shoes firmly planted on the rug, as if a force more powerful than his will held him down. The expression on his face was so devastatingly wretched I was transported back to the museum, and for several seconds, before I could bring myself to speak, I turned over in my head the portrait of Garshin. Then I saw what I hadn't before: a way to make everything that had ever gone wrong between me and Aeden right, to have him forget what I'd done; a way to secure his friendship, his company, his very presence in my life.

"I want Aeden to have equal contribution," I said.

Justin's first reaction was to laugh. His second, seeing that I was serious, was to look back at Aeden, staring at the wall behind me as though it were a place he wished he could be transported to.

"Please step outside for a moment," Justin told him.

Aeden stood up quickly. Before I knew it his chair was empty, and Justin and I were alone in the room.

"You realize the project will no longer be yours, but a joint venture. From the paper, to the mice, down to the very gene you discovered, you'll have to share everything with him."

"I don't mind sharing," I said. "Besides, Aeden deserves a break."

"This *is* his break, don't you get it? He has nowhere to go and nothing else in this lab to turn to. That was the whole point of calling his bluff."

"His mother suffers from anosmia, did you know that?"

"So do a million other people."

"I don't want him to feel humiliated."

"You think he's not?" Justin said. "You think he's pleased you stepped in to rescue him?"

"If he's not now he will be, eventually. We'll both be pleased."

"You must be insane," Justin told me. The look on his face, which I recall now as vividly as daylight, was of genuine alarm. "This isn't like you, Emily."

His presumption irked me. "So what is me, who am I, Justin?"

Justin seemed to have no answer for the question, not then anyhow. After a moment he pulled a small handkerchief from his breast pocket and began to dab the perspiration on his forehead. "I hope you realize the only thing in your favor is your surname."

"My surname?"

"It starts with an *A*. Apell *et al.*? Your name will be first on the paper. It will be the name people will refer to, the name on the byline. Or do you no longer care about that either?"

"I do," I said, unconvinced. "Sure I do."

Justin sighed. "Please don't tell me you didn't factor that in, Emily, before offering him equal contribution."

"Of course I did, Justin." But I hadn't. The thought of whose name would live on in the annals of history hadn't even crossed my mind. For better or worse I no longer saw the gene I'd discovered as a means to having my own lab, my independence, but as a bridge to Aeden.

———

WHEN AEDEN RETURNED TO THE ROOM, I COULDN'T TELL WHETHER he was pleased or not. His face was basically unreadable. He gave a furtive glance in my direction and lowered himself back down on the folding chair, where he sat with his arms crossed, watching Justin in a way that made me wonder if he was processing what Justin was saying. Even after Justin had finished congratulating him on his equal contribution status and moved on to discuss the work itself, how between him and me we would need to keep experiments running twenty-four seven if we expected to have knockout mice within a year in order to beat Craig to the punch—that is, if Craig hadn't published his results by then—Aeden seemed to be looking right through him.

It was only after about a half hour, after Justin had finally fallen silent and the meeting appeared to be over, or nearly over, that what was troubling him came to light.

"What about Allegra?" he asked.

"What about her?" Justin said.

"You left her out of the meeting. Isn't she also a part of this project?"

"Yes, please ask her to come here."

The person who followed Aeden into the room five minutes

later felt like a shadow of the Allegra Meltzer I'd coexisted with
for more than four months: the person who returned my good-
mornings looking anywhere but at me, and in the bathroom
washed her hands at cosmic speed, refusing to acknowledge me
even when it was just the two of us standing in front of the mirrored row of white sinks. Her elegant frame, usually straight as
a tack, was slightly sunken, and her hands senselessly spread on
her thighs. She sat down next to me on the couch, close enough
that I could feel the heat emanating from her body and smell the
residue of her deodorant. Her hair part was uneven, and thick
locks of chestnut hair covered the side of her face. I could see her
button nose and green eyes only in spurts, every time she nodded at Justin or raised her chin at him in what felt like an effort to
remain calm. Her lab coat had the yellow smear in the exact same
spot, and it occurred to me she hadn't laundered it in weeks.

Justin spoke to her at length, about my gene and the race
against the San Diego lab. In the quiet interlude that followed,
when it became apparent to everyone that Justin had basically
finished saying all he was going to say, Allegra unclasped her
hands from her knees and leaned into the table. "Can I take a
look?" She gathered the sequence pages carefully in her hands,
as if afraid to harm them, and settled the bundle on her lap.

She'd been sitting like that for a few seconds, with her head
lowered to the pages, when Justin embarked on an account of the
lab's expenses of the last three years. How the failed project had
cost him a small fortune and how he would have to keep a close
tab on the lab budget from now on, cutting corners where he
wished he didn't have to.

"Unfortunately," he said, "I can't afford to have three people
working on this project."

Allegra raised her head from a page. "She doesn't know the first thing about bench work," she said, speaking to Justin as if I weren't there.

"Of course she does," Justin said. "Don't you, Emily?"

Allegra turned her face to mine, meeting my eyes for the first time. She looked at me as if she expected me to acknowledge my shortcomings right then and there.

"Yes," I answered. "I have hands-on experience."

"We all have different talents," Justin said. "Not everyone is equally good at the bench. Are you or are you not capable of handling the workload?"

Aeden gave me a beseeching look from his chair. Though it was clear that Allegra's position in the lab was hanging by a thread, I was disinclined to help bring her on board the project. It had to do with Aeden, his friendship with her and my fear that if she stayed, there would be no room left for us, but also with the strong sense I'd always had in her presence of not fitting in.

I looked back at Justin. "Perfectly capable," I said, and from the corner of an eye saw Allegra gaze away from me forever.

THREE DAYS LATER SHE STOOD ON A SNOWY CORNER ON YORK AVE-nue and Sixty-Third Street. A taxi was parked at the bend of the street, and three years' worth of textbooks and folders and notebooks were packed inside its trunk. Aeden had carted the boxes down from the lab himself.

It had been threatening to blizzard all week, and finally it was: snowflakes falling from the milky sky at a dizzying pace, dimming the air and the sidewalk. Aeden's coat was fully unbuttoned and his head exposed. Allegra's coat, on the other hand, was buttoned all the way up to her chin, and on her head was a fur hat similar to the kind that Pavel in my father's lab had worn. She was holding a helium balloon—one of the several I'd seen floating around in the conference room that morning, where a going-away party I'd been careful to stay away from had been held in her honor.

After a while they embraced. From where I stood I could see the top of her hat just above Aeden's shoulder, the red balloon bobbing above them. The lab cart Aeden had used for the boxes, precariously parked on an incline, looked like it was about to roll down the street, all the way to the FDR Drive.

Suddenly, as if she could sense me watching them, Allegra raised her face to the research building across the street, all the way up to the floor of the lab. Instinctively I backed out of the window, though whether she had seen me, or had even been looking to see me, was anyone's guess. For all I knew, for all I know now, she was taking one last look at the place she'd come to three years earlier, full of hope, and walked out of empty-handed and burned out.

———

I NEVER SAW HER AGAIN, THOUGH I DO SOMETIMES IN MY DREAMS, a recurrent dream I've had on and off ever since I heard, from a reliable source, that Allegra had given up on science and was working as a patent agent in a law firm downtown.

In my dream the plane I've been traveling on has landed, and I emerge into a crowded airport terminal where I'm late for a connecting flight. I'm moving quickly, weaving my way with a heavy briefcase between throngs of passengers toward my gate, when I see her, a familiar speck in the sea of faces moving toward me, in the opposite direction. But it isn't until she has walked past me that I realize who she is. I turn around and begin to follow her. "Allegra?" I tap her shoulder with my free hand, but she continues to move, away from me. "It's Emily," I say, and in a louder voice, attracting bemused glances from an approaching wave of people: "Emily from the lab, don't you recognize me?"

She stops then, and turns around to face me, but the face I see as her eyes settle on me isn't hers. The face I'm seeing isn't one I'm able to recognize at all, until it dawns on me that I'm looking at my own.

PART THREE

RECOMBINATION

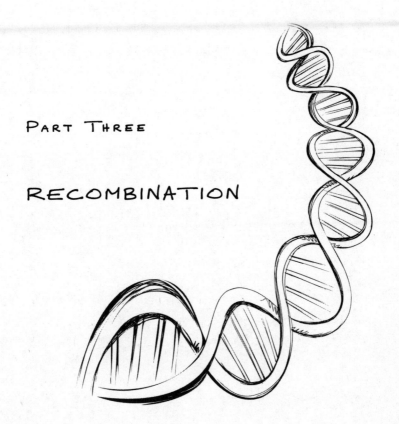

CHAPTER 14

THE FIRST TIME AEDEN SAW ME HANDLING A PI-
pette he walked away and for the rest of the
day did not speak to me again. Not that he'd been addressing me
with much more than monosyllables since our meeting in Justin's office. *I'll see you here again in an hour* were his usual words
for me, spoken to the timer in his hand, the water bath on my
workbench, my lab coat pocket.

About a week after Allegra left the lab we received a FedEx
package containing a DNA primer we'd rush ordered from a biological supplies company in Massachusetts. Aeden tore open the
dry-iced packet and stood the tiny vial in crushed ice alongside
an Eppendorf tube with buffer. I thought he would walk away, but
he didn't.

I reached for the stand of pipettes in front of me and pulled
out the thinnest one. I wrapped my fingers around the slender
neck and pressed the lever with my thumb and aimed the tip of
the pipette to the inner wall of the vial, raising the lever carefully to suck up all the liquid inside. The idea was to transfer it
to the Eppendorf and mix it with the buffer. Nothing too complicated, nothing I hadn't done before in summer lab rotations

and graduate school and in the lab when Aeden wasn't watching. But now he was. My hand shook, and instead of aiming the liquid into the tube I squirted it outside, wasting a pricey drop of DNA designed especially for our purposes. It rolled down the wall of the plastic tube like a tear and vanished into the ice. "I'm sorry," I said, and giggled, from sheer nervousness.

"You could have helped her stay," Aeden said.

It was the most personable thing he'd said to me in weeks, perhaps months, but by the time I raised my eyes to look at him, he, like the primer, was gone.

A week after the spill we went into the cell storage room at the end of the hallway to retrieve our frozen cells. We had screened a commercial library of bacterial cells containing genomic mouse DNA and had identified several cells that potentially contained my full-length gene. I had tinkered with the liquid nitrogen freezers before, lifted the heavy lids and reached inside them for the metal tiers of boxes. Those other times Aeden had alerted me to the pair of oven gloves hanging from the wall next to the freezers. But this time he didn't. I dipped a latex-gloved hand into the bubbling nitrogen, pulled out our tier, and, squealing in pain, managed somehow to release my frozen fingers from the metal handle. It plopped soundlessly back inside the freezer, shooting out a blinding mist of air.

Afterward, long after the fog had dissipated, I stood next to the freezer, holding my hands together.

"You okay?" Aeden asked me, in his smoke-roughened late-afternoon voice.

"Why didn't you remind me to wear the gloves?" I asked.

"I'm sorry," he said flatly. "The gloves are right in front of you."

Following the liquid nitrogen incident I came into the lab early one morning to check on the electrophoresis gel I'd left running overnight. By then Aeden and I were sharing the same bay. Justin had asked David to set me up in Allegra's former space to free up my bay for a new graduate student, and as much as I'd dreaded the idea of giving up the quiet solitude of my corner bay, I'd also felt a rush of excitement at the prospect of moving in with Aeden. Sitting back-to-back with me, he would have no choice but to talk to me, look me in the eyes, eventually make peace with me.

When he showed up that morning, later than usual, I was sipping cold coffee and reading *Introduction to Practical Molecular Biology*—one of several method books I'd taken with his permission from his shelf.

"You overslept," I said casually, despite the fact that it was nearly noon.

Aeden, who was in the habit of ignoring my attempts to make conversation with him, stopped in his tracks. But he wasn't looking at me. His eyes were on my workbench, specifically on the power supply box my gel was attached to. The amperage reading, I realized with a pit in my stomach, was higher than I'd thought. Much higher than it should have been.

"You let the DNA run out of the gel," he said, and headed toward his desk.

I staggered to my feet, reaching the bench in one move and lifting the gel tray with my bare hands and the electricity running. At the Eagle Eye machine across the aisle, where Aeden and Allegra had once stood together, celebrating their knockout mice, I pushed the tray into the slot and switched on the ultraviolet light, but instead of the glowing ladders of DNA I saw only a depthless black. The samples I'd loaded on the gel were lost, and the oversight would set us back at least a day.

I dumped the gel into the biohazards bin near the radioactive hood and walked back over to the bay. Aeden was sitting at his desk, staring at his laptop. I snuck a look at the screen and saw what I first thought was Earth viewed from a satellite. It took me a moment to realize I was actually looking at the olfactory bulb of a mouse, another to comprehend that Aeden was reviewing images of his knockouts. Quietly I sat on my chair, facing the empty desk wall in front of me. "I'm sorry, Aeden," I said, without looking at him.

"Sorry about what?" he asked.

I thought about it, and after a while said, "For being such a klutz?"

"You'll just have to redo the procedure."

It was still relatively early in the day, I figured if I set out to redo the DNA digests and rerun them on a gel, I could make up for the lost time, or partially make up for it. Instead of an entire day, only half a day would be lost. I sprang from my chair and hurried over to the end of the room where David was loading empty mouse cages on a cart. I opened the freezer and rummaged the shelves in search of the restriction enzyme box.

"Are you all right?" David asked me.

"I'm fine," I told him. I hadn't planned to mention my oversight with the gel, but being visibly agitated as I was, and having no one else to talk to, I did. "An accident, it's really nothing."

When I returned to the bay Aeden and I shared, I sat down at my bench and began labeling tubes for the digestion reactions. Minutes later David walked in. He was wearing a different lab coat, whiter than the one I'd seen on him earlier, and his hair, usually all over the place, was neatly parted to one side. "I can help you with those, Emily," he said, moving up to my bench.

"I didn't know you had so much time on your hands," Aeden said from his desk.

"I happen to have a couple of hours."

"No, you don't. You're just offering to help her because of the database. If there's a paper you want to make sure your name is on it for when you apply to med school. Hopefully they'll let you in this time around."

David's face reddened.

"So what?" I said, swinging my bench stool around to face him. "Why should it matter to you why David wants to help me?"

Aeden stood up. "If you want a technician, Emily, you're welcome to have one."

"I never said I wanted a technician."

Without a word he tramped past me with his laptop, and was out the door before I could say anything else.

After a wordless few moments David pulled Aeden's bench stool over to mine and sat down next to me. I looked at him and saw that his glasses were all fogged up.

"What a prick," he said, shaking his head.

"He's not," I said. "Please don't say that about him again."

————

AEDEN WAS GONE FOR THE REST OF THE DAY. THE NEXT MORNING he showed up in the lab earlier than usual, calm and collected in his long black coat, a Starbucks cup in his hand.

After checking his emails and finishing his coffee he stood up from his desk and pulled out a pair of latex gloves from the box on his bench and asked me if I needed any help.

It wasn't even a question.

After dismantling the southern blot on my bench I followed him to the radioactive hood in a corner of the room and stood with him behind a plexiglass shield, watching him expose the membrane of DNA to our radiolabeled probe, wash the membrane, and scan it with the Geiger counter in his hand, until the background radiation noise was narrowed to a piercing cry.

The sound came from somewhere in the upper left-hand side of the membrane. A spot we could not yet see. It wasn't until hours later, until we had exposed the membrane to an X-ray film and were standing by the developing machine in the darkroom, examining it under a weak yellow light glowing tenuously over our heads, that we were able to see it: the thick black band of DNA the probe had bonded with. It was located in a column of the film corresponding to colony two, indicating that bacterial cells from that colony contained my full-length gene. Now we could map out the entire gene and begin to make changes. I felt happier than I had in weeks, though it was only the first step in a very long process.

"It's a nice result," I said. "Isn't it?"

Aeden went on staring at the film, not answering me. At last he gave me a perfunctory smile and handed it back to me. "Why did you do it?" he asked.

"Do what?" I said, looking down at the film.

"Equal contribution," he said, in a lowered voice, as if afraid someone else might hear him. "You thought I'd tell Justin about the filing cabinet? I wouldn't have; that's not something I would ever do."

"I know," I said.

"And you know it's not like I had a string of job offers lined up outside the asshole's office. I hardly had any other choice but to stay here and help you."

"I know that also."

"So why equal contribution? It's your gene, after all. Not mine."

I stared up at him. I had imagined from the tone of his voice that he was indignant, but he wasn't, or at least didn't appear to be. In the scant light I thought I could see the flicker of a different, gentler sort of question in his eyes, and it gave me hope. "I wanted you to stay," I said.

"To make the mouse for you."

I shook my head. "It had nothing to do with the project."

"It didn't?" Aeden said uneasily. I could almost touch the disbelief on his face. "Then why did you want me to stay?"

"I don't know," I hedged.

"How can you not know?" His breath smelled of cigarettes and coffee, and of something faintly acidic that made me wonder if he'd had anything to eat all morning. "Why did you want me to stay, Emily?"

"I wanted to be with you, Aeden," I said finally. "I just . . . I just wanted to be with you."

CHAPTER 15

AFTER WHAT I TOLD HIM, AEDEN'S BEHAVIOR toward me underwent a slight change, discernible in his unfailingly saying hello in the morning and goodbye in the evening, steadying his eyes on mine when he spoke to me, and walking next to me instead of ahead of me on our way to the cell storage room, the equipment room, the cold room. Occasionally he would throw in an encouraging remark about my progress at the bench, going so far one day as to teach me how to hold a multichannel pipette.

"You're holding it like you're going to stab someone, Emily." He cupped my hand in his and veered it clockwise, readjusting it so that my fingers were aligned to one side of the instrument's neck and my thumb on the lever. "That's it." He released my hand from his grip and crossed his arms circumspectly across his sweater, a navy blue V-neck he'd taken to wearing lately. "Let's see you work."

Instead of eating in the conference room with the other post-docs, as he had been doing, Aeden began bringing his lunch into our bay. Usually he ate in silence, surfing the Internet while I recorded the morning's work in our notebook. But sometimes, especially if I was also eating, he would swing his desk chair around toward me and strike up a conversation about global warming, or politics, or what sort of sandwich I'd prepared at home and brought to work.

"So what's on the menu for today, turkey with cheese on rye or cheese with turkey on rye?"

"You think you're so funny," I said evenly, though I felt giddy with hope.

"My friends tell me I'm funny."

"I guess that makes us friends?"

"I guess it does," Aeden said, looking away from me, back at his screen.

In bed at night I often wondered what he'd made of my confession in the darkroom. After I'd told him what I had, he'd raised a hand up to his face and covered his eyes with it. I thought I even heard him say "Shit," and it made me wish I could take back my words. But as much as I regretted them, I was also relieved. I had nothing to hide from him anymore.

So it felt like we were headed toward a friendly reconciliation of sorts. Not that we were close to being friends: we were nothing but two people civilly working on the same project, sitting back-to-back in the same bay. Until there came a Sunday in mid-February when everything changed.

Sunday was the day of the week I looked forward to most. It was often just the two of us in the main room, surrounded by nothing but the murmur of machines. On this particular Sunday we'd been working on a northern blot all morning, screening various types of mouse tissue for the expression of my gene. We had about an hour to spare before developing the X-ray film, so Aeden suggested we go grab some lunch.

The day outside, despite the cold and the wind, was sunny, the kind of tender luminosity that comes with sound and smell and the seemingly unfiltered recognition of the person walking beside you. On our way back to the lab with our sandwiches I could feel Aeden looking at me, taking overt sidelong glances at me as I walked quietly next to him.

We had reached the campus when he asked me if I was seeing anyone.

"You mean a boyfriend?" I stepped ahead of him, through the gate.

"Yes, I suppose that's what I'm asking."

"Not at the moment, no," I said. "Why do you want to know?"

Aeden hurled the stub of his cigarette at the discolored lawn. "Tell me about him."

"My last boyfriend?"

"Yes."

I shrugged. "He was a medical student. I went out with him for a couple of months. We used to eat at his parents' every Sunday. Actually, it wasn't only his parents who were there but his entire family from Mumbai. The food was good but after a while I couldn't take the noise and the small talk and everyone asking me if I was feeling well, which I apparently wasn't." Aeden laughed. "Anyway," I said, laughing with him, "I don't think he was the right person for me."

"Why not?" Aeden asked, looking intently at me.

I wanted to tell him that while I'd been with Nirav—with every boyfriend I'd had—I'd never quite felt that I was being fully me. Instead I said, "Do you see me cooking for an army of people every weekend?"

Aeden gave me a long, pensive stare. "No, I guess I don't," he said.

While we ate our sandwiches at our desks I could feel him gazing absently at my jawline as I chewed, my mouth, the hollow of my neck. "What are you thinking about?" I asked.

"Nothing," he answered.

When the timer rang we walked over to the darkroom with the autoradiography cassette and shut the door behind us. The air inside the room was tight with the smell of vinegar. It always was, on account of the acetic acid in the developing solution, but I felt it more poignantly that afternoon. Or maybe I didn't. Maybe I felt it much later, recalling what happened.

The RNA imprint in our film was confined to olfactory bulb tissue, suggesting that the gene was exclusively expressed in the bulb, and though this did not necessarily mean that it had a role in smell, the result was encouraging. "It looks great," I said.

Aeden laid the film down on the developing machine and stretched his arm behind me. I imagined he was aiming to open the door and was surprised when instead he locked it and placed his hand on my shoulder. He turned me around until I stood facing him. I looked across the darkness at him, hardly seeing his face but feeling his thumb on my mouth, tracing the shape of my lower lip. He held my cheek in his hand, sandpaper dry and faintly smelling of cigarette, and with his other hand proceeded to unbutton my lab coat. "Are you okay with this?" he asked me.

"Yes."

We went to stand in a corner of the room, by a low table where discarded films were piled in translucent heaps. I let him undo my pants, and eagerly undid his. He swept the films aside and lifted me onto the table, leaning into me. I straddled him with my legs and locked my arms around his neck, drawing him closer, but when I tried to kiss him Aeden turned his face away.

Minutes later we were sitting in the main room again, back-to-back at our desks. A tremble lingered inside me, but I sat still as a mouse, pretending to tabulate our results into a notebook. I was waiting for him to say something, acknowledge what had happened, but he didn't.

I hadn't seen a movie in ages and was thinking of suggesting we go see one when Aeden stood up. I turned around and looked at him. He shouldered his backpack and opened his mouth to speak, but no words came out. Outside the window behind him it was already dusk, the bridge twinkling a weak and solitary light. "I can't be with you in that way, Emily, in the way that you would like. I thought I could, but I can't."

"I don't expect you to," I told him, and managed to smile.

It wasn't until hours later, after Aeden had left and I had returned home for the night and showered and stood in my pajamas and wet hair in front of the kitchen sink, drinking water from the tap, that I allowed his words to sink in, and felt something small, like a fissure, cracking open inside me.

———

LATER THAT WEEK WE WENT INTO THE DARKROOM AGAIN, TO DEvelop another film. Once again Aeden locked the door behind us and led me by the hand to the table in the corner of the room. It was early morning. A strip of sunlight fell through the crack beneath the door, slicing the floor in two: the dark side, where we were, and the bright side beyond the door. From our side of the room I could make out the drift of movement in the hallway, the transient sound of human voices. Again I tried to kiss him, and I felt the rasp of his chin on my forehead, and after a while, after we were finished, I smelled the sea-breeze odor of his T-shirt, in which my face was buried.

At noon I saw him in the conference room, having lunch with Steven. I couldn't hear what they were talking about, but by the looks of it, it seemed casual and intimate—the sort of exchange that happens between people who've known each other for years and will keep on wanting to know each other for years to come. I turned from the glass and headed straight to the women's bathroom, feeling a painful swelling in the back of my throat.

We returned to the darkroom again the following week, only this time without needing to. I willingly followed him across the hallway, into the room, and stood in the dark, watching Aeden latch the door. At the table in the corner I was anticipating the stroke of his thumb on my mouth, the odor of his skin, the soft feel of his shirt on my nose, but there was nothing like that this time; Aeden turned me away from him, pulled my pants down, and raised my lab coat up to my waist, steadying his hands on my lower back.

"No," I said.

"If it hurts I'll stop."

"That's not what I meant," I said.

He didn't ask me what I meant. He didn't need to. While it lasted, before he drew away from me and left the room and we avoided each other for the rest of the day, I shut my eyes and willed myself to be carried off, to a different place, from where I could see a light in the distance. But of course I couldn't. There was no light in the distance, only the humiliation of it all.

———————

FOR DAYS I COULDN'T MEET HIS EYES WITHOUT FEELING THAT AE-
den was seeing straight into my soul and basking in my disappointment. Whenever he spoke to me, which he did about work
exclusively, I found myself looking away from him, invoking the
impossible resolve to stay calm and behave as though I wanted
and expected nothing intimate or meaningful to ever happen
between us.

I ate lunch in my dorm room across the street, and dinner I
skipped altogether, leaving the lab at night as early as I could in
order to avoid being alone there with him. Weekends I came in
only half time, and usually only in the afternoon, when others
were likely to be there, buffering me from the sight of Aeden sitting at his desk with old images of his knockouts, and the sea-
breeze scent that felt like a stab in the heart.

For the most part this arrangement worked out well. While
the experiments ran smoothly I could do without Aeden's help
or assistance, relying only on the protocol sheets he handed me
each morning. Following his instructions I had made a dele-
tion in the gene that would prevent it from being expressed in a
mouse. Now I was looking to insert into the gene a marker that
would allow us to track it in embryonic stem cells. But this was
harder than I'd thought. I had screened hundreds of bacterial
colonies and failed to find a single one in which the gene and
marker were joined.

On that particular day, a week after our last encounter in the
darkroom, I sat hunched over a petri dish, my face to the swel-
tering flame of a Bunsen burner, maneuvering as best I could the
sterile toothpicks in my hand. I was picking clumps of bacterial
cells growing on the yellow lawn of agar and dislodging them one

by one into the wells of a microplate when Aeden stood up from his desk and walked over to my bench, standing close enough that I could smell him.

"Those aren't the colonies you should be picking," he said. "They're too big. You need to pick the slow growers; they're more likely to carry what you're looking for."

I went on picking them anyway, the snot-like colonies he was explicitly telling me not to pick.

"May I, please?" Aeden said.

Without looking at him I ceded my chair. Aeden took it and sat at my bench, scanning the hundreds of colonies in the dish with a scrutinizing frown. At last he aimed the toothpick in his hand at something I never would have seen: a colony that seemed to be barely there, its tiny head rising just above the surface of the agar. With a twist of his wrist he scraped it off the dish and dislodged it into the growth medium. "That's what you need to screen. In fact, your search might be over." He smiled at me, and I found myself meeting his eyes. "I'm sorry about the other day," Aeden said. "That won't happen again."

"No, it won't," I said, and just like that I felt the hurt melting away, and the hope I had somehow managed to bury renewed inside me.

The next day I walked into the darkroom with a dummy cassette and made my way with Aeden to the corner table. From then on I began to follow him around the lab again, and to play his game again, whenever and wherever he proposed to play it. We did it in the cell storage room, on the narrow strip of floor between the wall where the oven gloves hung and the nitrogen freezers. We did it in the equipment room, amid shakers with overgrown cells inside them and the smell of putrefaction, under the conference room table and on top of my desk to the sound of a night guard roaming the floor with his walkie-talkie. We did it wherever there was a door to shut and lock and lights to switch on or off, depending on his mood. We did it against walls, benches and desks, tanks and incubators, and on the linoleum floor. One moment I was light-headed and delirious and the next half-starved for what he could not give me and I was pretending I did not want or need. In my bed at night I fantasized about holding hands with him in a park, a movie theater; having a conversation with him where I saw clarity and warmth in his eyes.

"What do you want from me?" I once asked him.

"What do you want from me, Emily?"

One late evening, in the men's bathroom, I looked up at him from a kneeling position and watched his chest rise to a halt, and felt his grip on my hair dissolve. His eyes were shut against the iodine light of the stall. They remained shut for a long time, and I remember thinking it wasn't pleasure that he'd felt, and had been feeling all along, with each of our encounters, but the dissipation of a loss too painful to put into words: his wasted years in Justin's lab and his vanished youth, for at thirty-two he was no longer young, relatively speaking. Not young enough to start over again as a postdoc in another lab. Not young enough to start over from scratch, on his own project, on his own terms.

CHAPTER 16

N O ONE IN THE LAB APPEARED TO HAVE ANY IN-
kling of what was going on between us. In
public our interaction was limited to work, and in private we were
careful to bolt doors and stay away from windows, and to hardly
breathe. There had been talk on the floor of the head of the zebra
fish lab leaving his wife for his lab technician, and gossip about
the dean of admissions having sex with a graduate student in the
faculty club restroom. To be seen or heard by someone in the lab
would have meant a permanent stain on our standing as serious
scientists, serious people.

But then Justin saw us.

On a Sunday afternoon, in early spring, he had returned from
a conference and was unlocking his office door when we stepped
out into the hallway from the darkroom. My lab coat was hanging
in my arm and my shirt unbuttoned at the top. It must have taken
me several seconds to realize someone was actually there, standing some twenty feet to our right, because when I did, by the time
I caught sight of Justin staring at Aeden and me, he had turned
toward the frosted pane of his office door and pushed the door
open with his foot, letting himself and his carry-on through.

Minutes later he was in our bay. I had gotten into my lab coat
and was setting up a digestion reaction on my bench. Aeden was
sitting idly at his desk. In the past, the times Justin had shown up
in our bay to inquire about the project, Aeden had made a point
of ignoring him. Now he sat with his chair swiveled toward him
and a hand held across his unshaven chin, watching Justin with
unnerving interest, as if he were studying an animal in a zoo.

"What on earth have you been doing for the past four weeks?"
Justin asked, pacing the narrow space of our bay with his hands
behind his back and his eyes on the floor, as if the ruins there,
the scraps of aluminum foil and discarded pipette tips, might
shed light on what he'd witnessed. "When do you expect to have
mice?"

"Everything is going according to plan," I said, despite the
fact that we'd fallen considerably behind schedule, my focus having shifted from the staggering number of experiments running
simultaneously on my bench to the handwritten notes Aeden left
for me with threadbare information of where and when to meet.

"You expect me to believe that? You should be working out of
the tissue culture room by now and you're not. For all we know
the Levine lab already submitted their results." He wasn't looking at me. He hadn't even attempted to make eye contact with me.

"We're a little behind," I admitted. "It's no one's fault."

Aeden was smiling at the floor. I had a feeling he was about to
say something horrible, and he did. "What is it you want to know,
Justin?"

Justin stopped abruptly. "I beg your pardon?"

"Why are you here?"

"To check on your progress, why else would I be here?"

"That's not true."

Justin smiled at him, but I could tell he was ruffled. "You know better than I do why I'm here?"

"Not everything is in your control, Justin. Especially what happens behind closed doors."

"I don't know what you're talking about."

"Sure you do," Aeden said, stretching out his legs. "Maybe you don't want to admit it, but you know."

Justin turned away from him. I was hoping he would walk all the way out into the aisle and leave, but he didn't. He stopped in front of my bench and leaned into it, standing very quietly next to me. I had finished capping the tubes and was shakily inserting them into a floating rack inside the water incubator. I knew his conference had been in Iceland, because he had emailed the entire lab to let us know of his whereabouts, and because he'd sent me a private message saying how much he was enjoying the hot springs and how the smell of sulfur had taken him right back to his childhood in Saratoga, where his family had vacationed every summer. How this made him feel inexplicably calm and happy.

"How was Iceland?" I asked. It was all I could think to say. I glanced over my shoulder at him and saw his eyes fixed on a droplet of water on my bench. Before I could dab it with my lab coat sleeve he popped it with his thumb. Then he looked at me, and the look on his face seemed to be telling me I was no longer his partner in solitude. I had crossed a line. "Infernally hot," he said, and walked out of the room.

When he was gone I covered the water bath and saw the silver-tinged reflection of my face on the lid. My lips were thinner than I remembered them being, and my skin ghostly pale. My eyes had dark circles under them, from lack of sleep, I thought. But what grabbed my attention was the way they seemed suspended in a place that was neither here nor there, and contained a new sadness I had never seen in myself before.

"You realize not knowing is killing him," Aeden said behind me.

I turned away from my reflection. "I don't know why you had to provoke him like that. Nothing good will come of it."

"You honestly see things getting any worse for me?" When I didn't respond, Aeden shook his head and said, "It's been so easy for you, Emily."

"Easy?" I said, looking down at him. "You think it's been easy for me?"

"I think you've accomplished a great deal in six months, more than many scientists accomplish in a lifetime."

"I haven't accomplished anything yet, and that's not what I was referring to, Aeden."

"No? What were you referring to?"

"I'm referring to what's been happening between us."

"What's been happening between us?" Aeden echoed, as if he had no clue what I was talking about.

I looked away from him momentarily, trying not to cry. Then I said, "I'm talking about being with you and having to pretend for the rest of the day that I don't know you. Lying in bed at night hoping that the next time we're together you'll lower yourself to have lunch with me. I'm talking about . . ." Suddenly I felt I was drowning, it hurt so much to articulate what I'd kept inside for so many months, to even look at him. "I'm talking about feeling like no matter what I do, no matter how hard I try to get close to you, you will go on hating me."

"That's not true," Aeden said, looking shocked.

"Yes it is," I said. "You hate me for getting in your way, for discovering what you would have discovered had I never shown up in this lab."

The next thing I knew I had peeled off my gloves and was hurrying down the fire escape stairs to the ground floor exit. The air outside, despite the absence of any sun, was warm and moist and springlike. I thought I could even see tulips blossoming nearby and smell something of the sweet iron scent of cut grass that had sent me scrambling indoors as a child.

On the street, en route to my dorm, I saw the bridge to my left, its struts recalling the complex geometry of ridges inside the nose, where trapped airborne molecules bind to the receiving ends of neurons. Impulsively I turned left at the corner of the street and went up the ramp, across the overpass. The river beneath me gave off the mild stench of low tide, reminding me of enforced summer weekends on Lake Michigan with my father: the tedium of sitting on my strip of towel on a crowded beach, surrounded by people I didn't know, the crime of time passing in vain, of growing old.

On the promenade, where Aeden and I had convened in winter, nearly every bench was empty. I walked over to the nearest one and sat down on it. So much had happened since then; I had let so much happen. At what point during that short span of time had I allowed the shape of my dreams to be so altered?

I was gazing beyond the railing, at a ferry moving southward down the river, when I heard footsteps behind me, and turned to see Aeden descending the ramp. He came over to the bench and lowered himself down next to me, a white bundle in his hand. "You left your lab coat on the stairs."

I went on staring at the river, ignoring him. Aside from a few runners and people out with their dogs, we were alone on the promenade. The water at our feet was still, and the air silent. After a while I could make out the ferry under the bridge. "You'll never forgive me, will you?" I said. "For getting in your way?"

"It's not your fault," Aeden said. From the corner of my eye I could see him shaking his head. "You didn't get in my way, Emily."

"You would have found the gene. It's something I've often thought about, how if I hadn't gotten involved, you and Allegra would have tried your luck with David's library and eventually found it."

"I don't think so," Aeden said. His face was now turned to the water. "To tell you the truth, I highly doubt it. Three years ago there was no question in my mind that I would make an important contribution to this field, and I didn't, I haven't. Maybe it just wasn't in my cards to find your gene."

I looked at him. He was sitting with my lab coat pressed to his chest, wincing at the river. In the grainy light of dusk I could see folds in the skin of his eyes. I thought of the beach on Lake Michigan, of time passing in vain. "It's not my gene, Aeden. It's also yours. It's our pathfinder."

"Pathfinder, is that what you're calling it?"

I realized it was my first time telling him the name. "It's the name of a radar device used in boats, to aid in navigation. I looked it up on the Internet." Aeden was observing me closely, not taking in what I was saying as much as watching me speak. "What do you think?" I asked him. "About the name?"

"It's a good name, a fine name," he said. Then he took my

hand and wove his fingers between mine. "I want you to know I don't hate you, Emily. I never have. Far from it."

———

WE SAT LIKE THAT FOR A WHILE, HOLDING HANDS, HIS CHEST gently rising and falling, my heart jostling against my rib cage, threatening to fly out.

CHAPTER 17

T IME IN A RESEARCH LAB HAS A WAY OF EXISTING
    in notebooks and spreadsheets and dates re-
corded on the walls of flasks and vials and petri dishes; a way
of inhabiting its own dimension, removed from actual time. You
don't think in years or months, but in hours and minutes: you
think about this step, and the next step, and whatever happens
after is irrelevant. So long as you're on course, time seems to be
happening to someone else.

But then the trees outside look fuller, and the sun shines into
the rooms for longer periods of time, and it's not early March
anymore but April, and technically no longer winter, but spring
again. Another year has passed.

The spring I'm thinking of is punctuated in my mind by
the salty breeze blowing that afternoon from the East River,
stirring Aeden's dark hair away from his face as we sat on the
bench, holding hands. The second thing that marks the start of
that spring for me is what happened a few days later, one early
morning. Aeden called me in the lab. He'd never called me in
the lab, or anywhere else for that matter. When the landline of
our bay started to ring, I pulled away from the experiments on

my bench and hurried over to the black phone on the wall, and when I picked it up it was Aeden, asking me to meet him across the hallway in an hour.

The four narrow walls of the tissue culture room across the hall, where I had never set foot, were partitioned between three laminar flow hoods, a tall incubator and oxygen tank, a refrigerator and sink, and a wall-to-wall workbench with a view of the Chrysler Building. The bulky microscopes on the workbench, aligned in single file, resembled giant insects.

"Inverted microscopes," Aeden offered with didactic enthusiasm from the incubator. "You see the flip side of things." He produced a U-shaped flask from a shelf and brought it to the microscope nearest me, bracing the plastic base of the flask between two metal clamps and switching the stage lights on for me. I sat down at the bench and looked through the eyepiece. At the bottom of the flask, swarms of translucent spheres were bathing in a red liquid medium, like tourists on Mars.

"What am I seeing?" I asked.

"The electroporation results," Aeden said, sounding pleased with himself.

I looked up at him. "When did you do this?"

"I don't know, while you were sleeping, I guess?"

The plan had been to insert our modified gene into mouse embryonic stem cells after I was finished with all the preliminary analyses, but Aeden had gone ahead and done it earlier, at his own risk, making up for the lost time. I stared back down at the cells, in whose DNA our gene was now integrated.

It was obvious, but I wanted to say it anyway. "They're beautiful."

———

OF THE HUNDREDS OF CELLS FLOATING IN THE RED LIQUID ME-dium, only a small fraction were likely to have our gene inserted in the right location. To find them—the cells that had exchanged a copy of their normal pathfinder gene for our mutated one—we would have to screen the cells in the flask, and to screen them we'd have to expand them to colonies.

After only two days the cells were growing so quickly we were waking up in the middle of the night to replenish their growth medium, split them into new flasks, check the pressure of the oxygen tank to ensure the incubator was supplying enough oxygen to the cells. By the time we had finished everything we needed to do it felt pointless to go back across the street to our dorms only to have to be back again in the room two hours later. So with the first sign of dawn outside the window we went to the food truck across the street and got coffees and eggs on rolls to go. It was against lab rules to eat or drink inside the tissue culture room, but we did it anyway. We'd broken so many unspoken rules, this one hardly seemed to matter.

While we ate and drank we listened to music from Aeden's favorite radio stations, NPR news, and talk shows where people spoke a lot and said very little. But mainly, we listened to our voices. We talked nonstop. Except for that one conversation we'd had at the Tramway we'd never really spoken, and hardly knew anything about each other. Now we began to.

Over the weekend, Aeden told me, he'd tidied his dorm and gone shopping for a pair of new shoes and found nothing that he liked—nothing worth trading his shredded Converse sneakers for. He hadn't touched a cigarette in weeks, and wanted to start tennis again. "My brother and I used to play tournaments in high school. Do you play tennis?"

"I wouldn't know how to hold a racket," I said. "Besides, I'd much rather go to the gym."

"What gym do you go to?"

"I don't."

Aeden smiled at me, amused. "Why doesn't that surprise me?"

"I don't like crowds."

"You're in the auditorium every Friday."

"That's different," I said. "The lectures are different. There's a purpose to the lectures."

"There's a purpose to a gym, a concert hall, a football stadium. There's a purpose to being around other people, Emily."

I shifted away from him. "You're starting to sound like my father."

"Does that upset you?" he asked.

"Not at all," I answered, but it did.

His timer started beeping and Aeden stood up, and by the time he returned from the incubator with our tower of living cells, his mind was luckily in a different place, the conversation seemingly forgotten.

————————

WITHIN WEEKS THE BORDERS BETWEEN OUR CELLS HAD ALL BUT vanished, and amoeba-like colonies were starting to show themselves at the bottoms of the flasks. I was tired most of the time, but I'd never felt more alive than when we were there, just the two of us in the tissue culture room, drinking bad coffee at five in the morning with the city lights fading before us.

I'd discovered a theatrical side to Aeden I'd been completely in the dark about. One morning, quite out of the blue, he stood up from the workbench where we'd been sitting with the timer and ran a near-perfect imitation of Justin.

"Your Majesty." He bowed to some invisible king stepping through the door. "Let me help you."

"I can take off my own coat, Philip. Is that a mouse? I think I just saw a mouse scurrying into the kitchen."

"Oh no, I assure you there are no rodents in this household."

"But I just saw one, with my own eyes."

"Are you sure it wasn't the cook you saw, Your Majesty?"

"I think I can tell the difference between a person and a mouse, Philip, don't you?"

"I don't know, can you?"

"How dare you address me in this manner, Philip? You shall pack your trunk and leave at once."

"Gladly. Fuckhead."

It was a far cry from the less grandiose, more self-examining image I carried in my head of Justin, but I laughed nonetheless. With time Aeden perfected his role of the servant, and every time we stepped in and out of a room, even when there were people around, he would hold the door open for me and make a little bow as I walked past him. "Your Majesty," he'd say, and we'd snicker at our private joke.

When that joke was exhausted, we found something else to amuse us during the hours of waiting: Carlos, the guy from Lab Safety, never said good morning when he came to collect the trash, and the way he shook his head disgustedly at the mouse carcasses in the cold room was seemingly evidence enough that he hated his job. Aeden asked him once, as we sat in the tissue culture room, if he was all right. Carlos gave him an unfriendly grin and rolled his eyes indignantly at the large number of flasks popping out of the biological waste bin.

Aeden and I began to call Carlos "the reluctant stowaway," from the series *Lost in Space,* reruns of which, as it turned out, both of us had loved to watch as children. *The carcass bin is empty. I guess we missed chatting with the reluctant stowaway. Is that the reluctant stowaway at the end of the line? What is he feeding his muscles for lunch?*

The theme kept us busy for a good two weeks, until it too ran its course. By then, the end of April, a new graduate student from Boston by the name of Ginny Wu had moved into my old bay, and we often found ourselves discussing her.

From the smell of the hallway alone it was possible to know whether Ginny was in the lab. She wore a singular perfume with a note of citrus that carried a repulsive undertone, similar to rotting fruit. Aeden was so baffled by the duality of her smell that he came up with a theory to explain it: a dab of perfume was perceived as pleasant because it activated unique targets in the olfactory bulb, whereas a surplus recruited extra ones, resulting in the distortion of the scent.

"What do you think?" he asked.

We were sitting side by side at the hoods, picking our first batch of colonies. I was having a hard time using the pipette in my hand with the right precision, and had shredded several potentially precious colonies to pieces. "It's plausible. The question is how to test it."

"We should figure out a way," Aeden said.

"We should," I agreed, but my thoughts had drifted to Ginny. "Someone should advise her to stop wearing so much perfume."

"Maybe you'll take the plunge."

"She would despise me for that."

"You're probably right," Aeden said. "Maybe Steven should tell her." I shot him a questioning look. "He likes her, you know."

"Steven likes Ginny?" For all her good looks and chirpy disposition and the rumor that she was a professional oboist who gave charity concerts in her spare time, I thought there was something disquietingly dull about Ginny, something that brought to mind a hollow tree where a woodpecker might go nest.

"Not just Steven." Aeden aimed his pipette at another colony. "Everyone in the lab has a crush on Ginny, smell and all."

"You too?" I asked him, my heart skipping a beat.

Aeden shook his head. "I think I'd be bored out of my mind with her."

CHAPTER 18

THE HALLWAY OUTSIDE AEDEN'S DORM, ON THE uppermost floor of the building, was the mirror image of mine several stories below: chain-link-patterned carpeting of a purplish unmemorable color, and twelve apartments facing west instead of east. Long drapes sheathed the two windows of his studio, and a large rug covered the bare wooden floors I'd never bothered to conceal. A prefab bookcase stood opposite the two windows, its shelves replete with books and magazines and music and photo albums. His bed, in a corner of the room, wasn't a sofa bed like mine, but a proper one, queen-size with a headboard and a frame supported by four legs coated in aluminum.

On the surface we went there to have lunch while our cells grew, but mainly we went there to be together. We bought food in the cafeteria and sauntered with our Styrofoam boxes out of the campus, as if we were headed to a park nearby, only to leave the boxes on his kitchen counter while we went through the motions. But the motions lacked the mindless assuredness they'd had in the darkroom, the cell storage room, the equipment room, and conference room of the lab. We kissed awkwardly, avoiding each other's eyes like teenagers, and not lingering in his apartment any longer than necessary. In a way, it was as if what had gone on between us inside those rooms had stripped us of any pureness of feeling we would have had had our relationship started out on a different note.

But then late one evening, as we were wrapping up our experiments in the tissue culture room, Aeden casually invited me to his place for dinner. We ordered Indian food from a local restaurant, and after dinner sat in his kitchen drinking tea he'd prepared from a loose stash of Darjeeling leaves his mother had mailed him from New Jersey. It was my first time there outside working hours, without any other purpose but to be there, and I was basking in the moment, elatedly focused on the song playing from the main room, the sweet tea in my mouth, his bare feet under the table, the confidential tone of his voice telling me about his mother.

"What worries me is she's lost a ton of weight. That's what my dad tells me. She claims she's on a diet but I know that she's depressed. There's no joy in her voice unless the kids happen to be around. My brother has two boys. Mark and Mitchell."

"Mark, I've heard you talking about him on the phone, with your mother. Do they live near her?"

"Same neighborhood."

"That's very lucky for her. I mean, for you too, I'm guessing."

Aeden sighed. "Yeah. I should go visit her." I waited for him to tell me more about his mother, his family, but he didn't. "What about you, Emily? When was the last time you saw your mom?"

"I've never seen her," I said without thinking.

Aeden stared at me across the table. "What do you mean?"

"She left me with my father when I was three months old. That's really all I know about her."

When I met his eyes again Aeden was studying me with a barely contained look of alarm on his face. "Has she ever tried to get in touch with you?" he asked, making an effort to sound casual about it.

"Not that I know of."

"Have you ever tried to get in touch with her?"

"I don't even know her name."

"Can't you find out?"

I shrugged. "She worked in my father's lab for a while, so I suppose I could, but I don't want to."

"How could you say that? She's your mother."

I stood up from the table and left the kitchen and went to the bookcase, where I stood taking in the soothing and familiar names on the spines of Aeden's CD collection, his books and jacketed photo albums. I recalled the floating rack of used petri dishes on his bench, some of them so old the agar inside them had peeled off like a shoe sole, his collection of old sweaters and shoes, and I realized, for the first time, that what passed through Aeden's hands was seldom ever trashed, that he clung to time, kept close track of the past. I picked up one of the albums from the shelf and flipped through it and felt lighter on my feet. It was a family album I imagined his mother had assembled, with pictures of Aeden dating back to his childhood: images of him and his brother shot on a ski lift, in a Mayan ruin, at a sandy beach with the sun sinking behind them. I heard a sound and saw Aeden standing some ten feet away, gazing awkwardly at me.

"I should leave," I said.

I returned the photo album to the shelf and was beginning to make my way to the door when he started toward me. I was expecting him to pull me down to the rug to do there what we'd done an hour earlier, but he held my face in his hands and kissed me, and kissed me again, and again, and again.

———

I DON'T KNOW PRECISELY HOW LONG IT TOOK FOR AEDEN AND ME to be together, in the way that couples are together. I know it must have happened some two to three weeks after that night in his dorm, because the days outside were consistently warmer and the campus grounds lime green and redolent with the smell of grass.

We had screened hundreds of colonies without finding a positive one, and then one day we found it. The X-ray film spat out of the developing machine with a scraping sound and fell into my hands, infusing the darkroom air with a fresh new dose of acetic acid. In the darkness I could see something jutting out of the sea of monotone lanes: a lane with two bands of DNA instead of one.

I can't remember anymore what lane number it was, or what colony number of the hundreds we'd screened, or whether it was Aeden or I who picked it. I only remember the imprint of a band showing itself beneath another band, like an added rung in a ladder, and thinking to myself that it wasn't real.

Aeden tugged the film from my hands and raised it to the light. "There it is," he said, pointing at the faint band and running his finger across it, as if to confirm that it was there. "Our gene instead of the original."

Hours later, after pizza in his dorm and several bottles of Corona in celebration of our milestone, I awoke in his bed to the hum of something electrically powered. The air conditioner was on and the curtains were drawn over the windows. I didn't know what time it was but guessed that it was closer to night than to day.

Aeden was lying next to me. His eyes were closed, and he was breathing with a whistling rasp that led me to believe he was still asleep. I quietly left the bed and tiptoed over to the kitchen, where I pulled a bottle of Perrier out of the fridge and drank the water straight from the bottle, a liberty I'd never taken with anyone.

When I stepped back outside Aeden was awake, his head propped on a pillow.

"I thought you were sleeping," I said, from the kitchen entrance.

In the frail light I could see him gazing with curious intensity at my breasts, my hips and thighs, my pubic hair, my feet. After a pause he said, "You're beautiful, Emily."

I ran over to the bed and fell into his arms and we lay there for a while. My ear was pressed to his chest, and I could feel his heart beating, and in between the beats a distant murmur that was like a language of its own. "We need to head back to the lab," I said.

"I wish we could just stay here," Aeden replied. He gazed down at me, and when our eyes met I felt something pass between us: a longing that I'd never before felt from him.

"So do I," but then I stood up from the bed and began to get dressed. The cells with our mutated pathfinder were in the incubator, and we needed to go check on them.

PART FOUR

CHIMERA

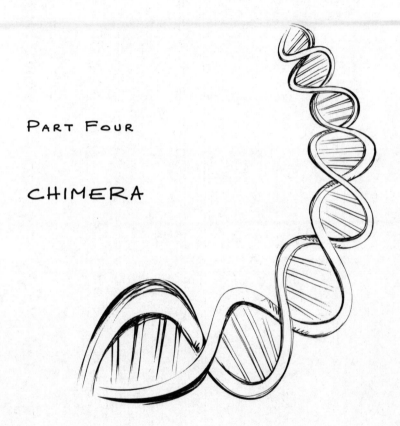

CHAPTER 19

W E DELIVERED OUR CELLS TO THE ANIMAL FA-
cility, where a technician injected them into
growing mouse embryos. One of the embryos developed into a
male with brown cow-like blotches in his fur, signaling the possible presence of sperm in his body derived from our mutant
cells. The chimeric male had grown and fathered two knockout
mice, which we'd crossed to each other, and whose offspring we
planned to analyze.

With more time on our hands than usual, Aeden and I were
often up in the terrace of our dorm building, on clear summer
nights, aiming to see Jupiter with the makeshift telescope he'd
built out of cardboard. I kept a spare toothbrush in his bathroom
cabinet and a change of underwear in one of the sliding drawers of
his closet. Weekend mornings we slept in late and had breakfast
in his kitchen, listening to music and discussing without inhi-
bition everything from testing his theory about smell distortion
to the futility of attempting to see anything other than Orion's
Belt with his telescope to the blatant fact that we were living in a
dorm and it would have been nice to have more space. I recalled
my conversation with Justin at the restaurant in December and it

felt odd, as though it had been another person speaking instead
of me. I did envision another way of life for myself, despite what
I had told him. I had often thought about what it would be like to
be with someone for the long haul, and to have children with that
person. But I had never exactly thought about it in that way, or in
that particular order. What came to mind when I thought of it,
the only thing that actually came to mind, was a woman with her
hands deep in her coat pockets, waiting on a snowy street corner
similar to the one where my father had waited for me when I was
little, for the school bus to arrive. It was a transient image, about
as faint and seemingly unreal as the band in our X-ray film. But
the woman on the street corner had resurfaced in my head that
summer more often than she had during my entire life.

As the summer passed, though, I often found myself steering
our conversation toward the project, away from Aeden's growing
tendency to complain about being confined to a university dorm
at his age and unable to afford a car while people like his younger
brother—for whom the word *cell* meant nothing but a phone—
were living in houses large enough to fit tennis courts into, and
replicating themselves.

"How many kids do you want to have?" he asked me.

Until then I'd been enjoying the poached eggs on country
white bread crisped to a golden brown he'd expertly prepared.
"Two," I said, and made a fleeting victory sign with my free hand.
I didn't know where the number had come from, and wasn't entirely sure about wanting to have children, but his assumption
that I did made me confident enough to believe that I could.
"What about you?"

Aeden nodded appreciatively at me across the table, as if we
were talking about a routine procedure in the lab, known to us

both for its uncomplicated beauty and unfailing reliability. "Two is a good number, I suppose, a manageable number."

————————

TWO WEEKS LATER, ON LABOR DAY, I WAS RIDING A TRAIN WITH him to Livingston, New Jersey. Outside our car window, suburban little streets with telephone poles had given way to flat open fields such as I hadn't seen in almost a year. It was a clear, hot, sunny day, one of those breezeless silvery September days when even the air feels treacherously raw and alive. My mind kept anxiously wandering back to the snapshots that had been running obsessively through my head for weeks, ever since Aeden had announced that he wanted to introduce me to his parents: images of planting a kiss on his mother's cheek, shaking hands with his father, sitting down to build a puzzle with five-year-old Mark. I had no experience with children and had never gotten along with families, much less mothers of boyfriends, but then I had never really cared to until then.

"I like your dress, Em," Aeden said. He'd started calling me Em, instead of Emily. "And the heels." It was his third time commenting on my sandals. "You should wear heels more often."

"Heels are a pain to walk in."

"You look good in them."

"I've had these forever," I said, though I had in fact rush ordered the sandals, along with the sleeveless summer dress I was wearing, from a Macy's catalogue in my regular pile of junk mail. The fields outside the window were starting to disappear, and the landscape to dot with concrete, signaling our imminent approach to Livingston. "I hope your family likes me, Aeden."

Aeden leaned forward in his seat and tucked a loose strand of hair behind my ear. "I think they'll dislike you as much as I do," he said, and planted a kiss on my forehead.

AT THE STATION THERE WAS NO ONE TO GREET US. AEDEN STOOD for a moment by the doors, checking his phone for missed calls. There were none. He dialed his brother's number and when no one picked up muttered "Idiot" under his breath. Then he shouldered his backpack and led me across the street, past the waiting vehicles, to a line of taxis. In truth I was almost relieved to climb into the anonymity of the cab's back seat, to put off the introductions a few more minutes.

His childhood home, a redbrick Tudor lined by tall trimmed hedges, recalled in a loose sort of way the small house I'd grown up in. Parked in the driveway were two cars, one of them a Jeep so painstakingly polished I could practically see our reflection. We walked past it, along a juniper-bordered path curving up to the main entrance of the house, where a wide wooden door stood ajar.

The inside of the house smelled pleasantly of smoked wood, and faintly of pressed flowers, onions, a chicken roasting in an oven. In the den a young guy with a babyish face who looked nothing like Aeden sat on an easy chair, watching a tennis match on TV. Aeden thanked him ironically for picking us up at the train station, to which his brother confidentially rolled his eyes at me, as though we were best friends, and said something to Aeden about a car that I failed to catch.

I left them arguing in the den and wandered past the living area, along a narrow passageway, into a large open kitchen, where a wire-thin woman clad in a cocktail dress stood absurdly in front of a chopping board, slicing onions. "You must be Rose," I said, recognizing Aeden's mother.

At first she didn't hear me or seem to notice me standing there in front of her. "You must be Rose," I said again, and watched her raise her face from the chopping board. Her eyes were light gray, like Aeden's, and when the recognition of who I was settled in, she smiled at me, and I saw the woman on his desk wall in the lab. "I'm Emily. Thank you for having me."

She put down her knife and shook my hand with surprising vigor. "A pleasure to meet you, Emily. I feel I almost know you. Aeden does nothing but talk about you."

"What has he said?"

"Everything."

"Everything?" I wondered if he'd told her about the filing cabinet incident, and found myself almost wishing for some reason that he had.

"Well, obviously not everything," Rose said. "Aeden wouldn't..." She was studying me now, and there was a familiar look in her eyes, as though she were staring through thin ice into a clear pond, seeing strange and unexpected life forms scurrying within her field of vision. "Monica," she called out. "Monica, this is Emily Apell, from the lab?"

Monica, whose presence I'd been only vaguely aware of until then, along with that of her two children, smiled curiously at me from her cross-legged position on a floor mat. A small boy in diapers was tugging at her shirt in a way that made me wish she would ask him to stop. The older boy, who I assumed was Mark, sat at a little plastic table nearby, quietly drawing. "Good to meet you, Emily," Monica said, and gazed neutrally at Rose, as though I'd passed a test of some sort.

"How about some lemonade?" Rose asked.

———

SHE LED ME INTO A SUNROOM WITH A LOFTY CEILING AND TALL windows through which the sky was visible. A pitcher of lemonade and a platter of frosted cupcakes stood at the center of a white coffee table, between two white couches. Rose sat, and I sat next to her, looking out to a quadrangle of hedges lining a lawn mown to a carpet-like texture. There were no trees anywhere in sight, no high branches swaying in the untouched wilderness I'd imagined. In a paved area, not far from where Rose and I sat, a tall man in his sixties was unhurriedly flipping steaks on a grill. He looked like an older, somewhat sedated version of his son. Aeden thirty years from now, I thought with unease.

Rose filled my glass with lemonade and patted my knee. "Drink up, don't be shy," she said, though I wasn't being shy. Then she said, "About the project, Emily, I want you to know that I hold nothing against you. You went to the lab with a purpose, and you're accomplishing exactly what you set out to do. I admire that."

"Aeden is too," I said. "We're working together."

"Smell research." She blinked as if the light in the room was suddenly irking her. "I was always opposed to it. Aeden had a wonderful future ahead of him, and he gave it all up, after the accident. His work at Princeton was in immunology. I don't know if he ever told you."

"He doesn't like to talk about that," I said, which was true. The times I'd asked Aeden about his graduate work he'd been almost too quick to describe it as a dead-end street.

"That's because he never should have gone to New York," Rose said. "I advised him not to, but it got into his head to switch fields, and when something gets into Aeden's head you might as well give up trying to reason with him." She poured more lemonade into her glass. "At any rate, I'm glad it's nearly over."

"Not for another two years," I said. "After we analyze our knockouts we'll start searching for more genes. If our gene is important it's possible that there are others like it, maybe an entire family."

Rose looked suddenly confused. She lifted the pitcher and asked me if I wanted more lemonade, which was strange because my glass was nearly full. "How about trying one of my famous cupcakes, Emily?" she said, with the pitcher gripped in her hand.

"They look delicious," I said, and to humor her: "Aeden raves about your cooking."

We sat on the couch for a while, sharing a rich chocolate cupcake I was sorry to hear might as well have been mud in Rose's mouth, and chatting about her short-lived career as an anthropologist. She missed being out in the field, she said, the sun on her face, using her mind. But she had no regrets. She'd realized shortly after having Aeden that family was more important than work, career, or any kind of discovery. Wanting to steer the conversation to a more familiar topic, I explained how Aeden and I had inactivated the pathfinder gene in embryonic stem cells, how a technician had injected them into mouse embryos and implanted the embryos into a female, how a chimera had been born that had luckily fathered a male and a female knockout, who'd recently given birth to a litter.

"Chimera," Rose mused, interrupting my train of thought. Her eyes had been fixed on my hands, which I moved for emphasis as

I spoke. "Isn't that also an unrealizable dream, something that is hoped for but impossible to achieve?"

"I didn't know that," I offered, wondering how this was relevant to what I was telling her. "My point is, Rose, we're nearly there. In a few weeks we'll analyze the litter, we'll know the result of our experiment."

"Wonderful," Rose said, but I could tell I'd lost her.

Aeden came into the room then, and she jumped up from the couch to greet him. They stood by the door, about five feet away from me, hugging each other in a way that made me think of a mother bear and her overgrown cub in the wild. Rose was nearly as tall as Aeden, but many pounds lighter.

At last Aeden stepped back from Rose, looking her over. "You look great, Mom."

Rose pursed her lips. "Don't lie to me."

"You do," Aeden said, and, making meaningful eye contact with me, "Doesn't she, Em?"

That Rose Doherty looked great wasn't exactly true. Her skin tone was blotchy and her cocktail dress hung from her frame like a curtain. On her feet were bedroom slippers, instead of the ladylike shoes I'd been envisioning.

"You don't need to lie, dear," she said. "I know I'm all skin and bones."

"You just need to put on some weight, Rose," I said. "That's all."

"Thank you, darling. I appreciate your frankness. I really do." She turned to Aeden. "Your Emily here is an interesting girl."

I felt a little chill in my spine. The word *interesting,* I knew, wasn't genuine.

"I had to practically force her out of the lab," Aeden told her.

He walked over to the couch I hadn't had a mind to stand up from and sat down next to me.

Rose sank into a nearby chair. "So you stole her from the lab?"

"Rescued her is more like it," Aeden said, taking my free hand in his.

"That's a lie," I said, though it wasn't exactly a lie.

"No, it's not." He took the glass of lemonade I'd been holding on to and settled it on the table. "If it weren't for me, she would be there right now, perusing databases on Labor Day."

"He's exaggerating," I told Rose with a smile, trying to blot out her *interesting*.

"You don't know the half of it, Mother," Aeden said. "You've never met anyone like Emily in your life."

"I'm sure I haven't," Rose said, smiling politely at me.

We sat there for about an hour, discussing neural regeneration and how Rose's olfactory bulb might eventually heal to allow new nerve endings to migrate into it and connect to their targets, how it was still possible, despite the dim future forecast for her, that she might be able to smell again one day. As I was trying to convince her of this I caught Aeden gazing thankfully at me, and for a little while, before we sat down at the table to have lunch, I felt I almost belonged there, in that room, in that house, with him and his mother and the rest of the family.

The way it felt, when I remember it now, was as if I was breathing borrowed air.

————

THE DINING ROOM TABLE WAS SMALL, AND WANTING TO BE SOCIABLE I had taken the empty chair between the toddler and Aeden's father, Robert. Aeden was sitting directly across from me, between

Rose and his brother, Matthew. On the other side of the toddler's high chair, where I could not see them, were Mark and his mother, Monica. The air inside the room was stuffy with wall-to-wall carpeting and the smells of cooked food. My attention kept wandering off to the console table by the wall with its family pictures, the different versions of Aeden's former self.

Aeden's father, a retired civil engineer, poured wine into my glass. "So what does this bridge motif of yours do?" he asked me.

"We don't know," I said. "We don't know what conformation the motif acquires in the protein, or what it's doing, but I like to think it's doing something special." I forced down a few gulps of the wine, knowing that the alcohol would make me more open to conversation.

Across the table Matthew was talking with the authority of an expert about car leasing deals. Aeden was nodding at his brother, apparently listening to what he was being told, but I could tell by the anxious looks he kept shooting in my direction that he wanted the conversation to end. That's when his brother said: "You'll need to have a car if you move out there."

"Move where?" I asked.

Matthew looked at me. We'd been introduced but hadn't exchanged more than two words. "You don't know?" He looked back at Aeden. "You haven't told her?" His eyes shifted with interest between the two of us.

"Cambridge, Massachusetts, dear," Rose offered from her chair.

An image formed at that instant in my head, crisp as the day outside. I don't know what prompted it, or how it came to be that I immediately put two and two together, but there it was: a small footbridge connecting two brick buildings across a narrow waterway. "Is that the place you were browsing the other day on your laptop?" I asked Aeden.

He brought his hands up to his face and rubbed his eyes. "It's a biotech company. I have a job interview."

"You already have a job," I said.

"What job?" Rose said. "Four years laboring in that man's lab. You call that a job?" She was holding her fork to her mouth as if she'd been feeding herself all along, when she hadn't even touched her food. I remember hating her at that moment.

"Why didn't you tell me, Aeden?" I asked.

Aeden lowered his hands to the table. "I only found out about the interview last week," he said.

"I'm talking about you wanting to leave."

"I'm not going anywhere for certain, Emily. Besides, you can't blame me for wanting out."

I knew I should stop talking about it, but I couldn't help but say, "I wish you had told me this before, instead of now, here."

"You're right. I should have. I'm sorry," he said uncomfortably.

To clear the atmosphere, or maybe because he genuinely wanted to know, Robert asked, "What are you going to do afterward, Emily?"

"Afterward?" I said.

"What are your plans for when the project is over?"

"Emily isn't your ordinary scientist, Dad," Aeden said, looking with pride at me. "She wants to have her own lab."

I met his eyes and felt something sharp wedged inside my chest.

"That's very ambitious," his father remarked with enthusiasm. "Have you always wanted to have a laboratory of your own?"

"Yes," I said, and realized how utterly true this was.

The toddler next to me was whining from his high chair, pointing at a cup lying at my feet. I remembered being older than him and unable to speak, a woman taking care of me and a boy peeing in my orange juice, getting into a fight with someone whose arms were the width of my thigh and clinging to the woman's necklace, white pearls in my fist spilling all over the floor. I remembered my father examining the bruise on my head and never seeing the woman or her family again. I remembered, after that, my father standing at the corner of our street in Shaw Woods with his arms crossed to his chest, waiting for the school bus to drop me off.

"What about a family?" It was Rose's voice.

"What?" I said. For a moment I wanted to think she was referring to the family I'd told her about, having to do with the gene, but of course that's not what she meant.

"Don't you want to have children?"

"No." I picked up the plastic cup off the floor and handed it back to Mitchell.

"No?"

"No."

"She doesn't really mean that, Mom," Aeden said.

"Yes, I do," I said, feeling suddenly fed up with the whole pretense. "Motherhood is overrated, if you ask me. Human company is overrated."

The silence that followed this last statement was so acute I could hear someone talking in the den, where Matthew had left the tennis match running. Rose was no longer looking at me. No one was except for Aeden, who was inexplicably smiling at me, as though I'd made some subtle kind of joke whose meaning he alone had understood.

"Any news from Allegra?" his mother asked him.

I lifted my glass off the table and downed the rest of the wine.

———

THE NEXT HOUR I SPENT MAKING AN EFFORT TO EAT THE thousand-layer cake Monica had graciously offered me a slice of and helping Rose clear the table, moving in a mindless state of inebriation between the dining room and the kitchen. On one of my returns to the kitchen I paused by Mark, who was at his makeshift table with an origami book, folding strips of colored paper with his hands. I had entertained the idea of sitting with him, but all I could do was stand there with my tray and watch. He raised his head and gave me a fierce funny look, as if to let me know he knew that I was there. "Are you still mad at my uncle?" he asked.

"I wasn't mad," I said.

"I like your hair."

"Why?"

"It's different."

"How?"

He shrugged. "Just different."

"I like that airplane you're building."

"It's not an airplane," he said. "It's a swan."

When I returned to the dining room Robert was unfolding a crumbling road map on the table. Aeden was in the den. I could hear him laughing, and Mitch egging him on. Then he came into the dining room and walked up to me and asked me if I wanted to go for a walk. His father raised his head from the map he'd been studying and looked at me. "Or you can drive out east with me," he said. "I'll take you on a sightseeing tour of the Bayonne Bridge.

In honor of your soon-to-be-celebrated molecular bridge," he added without irony.

I smiled at him, and shook my head.

"You should go with him, Em," Aeden encouraged.

"C'mon," Robert told me. "Put that stupid thing down." Meaning the tray in my hands. "We'll have a good time."

He was an ordinary-looking man, with a balding head and a sweet smile, one of those people you sometimes end up wishing you'd gotten to spend more time with. But I turned the offer down. I don't remember exactly what excuse I ended up giving him. I may have told him I was tired and wanted to go upstairs and rest, which was true. The larger truth, however, was that I wasn't feeling up to it. But as things turned out, I might have been better off going on that sightseeing tour with Robert, disappearing from the house for a couple of hours and forgetting that Aeden was looking to leave the lab. And forgetting also what I'd said about human company.

CHAPTER 20

AEDEN'S ROOM UPSTAIRS IN THE ATTIC WAS peaceful and quiet, with a low, slanted ceiling and the clean smell of wood. The single bed by the window and a bare desk set up against a wall were its only furnishings, and the only decoration a poster of Gwen Stefani that I imagined had been on the wall since Aeden's high school days. I unstrapped my aching feet from the sandals and walked barefoot across the cool plywood floor, over to the bed. The window at the foot of it looked out onto the same backyard I'd seen from the sunroom on the ground floor, but from up here I could see beyond the property line trees from neighboring houses, and shaded patches of ground.

A memory I'd thought buried came to me as I sat there: an oval hole in a dead oak tree, bright sunbeams trickling sparingly across the hole, disintegrating to needles on their descent to the ground, where my father and I sat in the snow, on a fallen tree limb, trying not to make a sound. If we as much as coughed, he warned me, the woodpecker would not come out of his hole to feed.

In the snow-muffled air I could hear tree branches creaking with the weight of the snow, and, faintly, the sound of the wind,

though the air did not seem to move around us. The clearing
where we sat was hushed and still and quiet in a way that felt
like an invitation to stay there, in that human-free world, forever. It occurred to me I'd never felt happier in all my life, and
with this came a strange and troubling truth: for no apparent
reason, I didn't like people very much, and did not care to be
around them.

That's when I opened my mouth and shouted, to my father's
consternation. The sound of my voice reverberated across the
forest and returned to me unscathed. I shouted again, louder,
and my voice rose and lingered somewhere high above the can-
opy and returned again. Over and over again I shouted, and the
more I did, the sooner my voice came back to me, as though it had
never left. I knew then that I belonged in the world, despite what
I felt, or failed to feel. I was a part of it, like everyone else was.

I never did see the woodpecker, though.

I rested my head on Aeden's pillow and closed my eyes, and
then I must have dozed off for a long time, because when I opened
them the light was fading, and there was an irking pressure in
my bladder. I remembered the small restroom on the landing,
at the bottom of the steep staircase leading up to Aeden's room,
and stood up from the bed and walked out. Descending the stairs
I heard voices, and realized that Aeden and his mother were
downstairs. Not on the landing, but a staircase farther below,
in a small sitting area I'd walked through earlier, on my way up
to his room. I was moving slowly down the near-vertical flight
of stairs, trying not to eavesdrop on their conversation, when I
heard Rose say something that made me stop. "Overrated. She's
certainly not the most sociable animal in the room."

"To tell you the truth, I like that about her."

"It doesn't bother you she didn't crack a smile at the baby? The whole time she was sitting next to Mitch she may as well have been sitting next to a wall."

"She's not used to having kids around."

"If I may say so, Aeden, something about her feels a little off. There's a name for what she has. You don't need to be a psychologist to know—"

"There's a name for what everyone has. You think you and Dad and everyone else around here are perfectly normal?"

"Sit down, please, I'm not done."

"Then stop putting labels on her. You don't know the first thing about her."

"You wanted my opinion."

"Forget I ever asked. I must have been crazy to bring her here."

I remember wanting at this point to turn around, burrow myself in Aeden's room, forget what I'd heard Rose say about me, but something held me in place.

"You obviously get along with her. You might even love her. I can see it in your eyes, the way you look at her. But people like Emily don't need other people."

"You don't know the first thing about her."

"It's true I don't, but I know you, and I know she won't make you happy, not in the long run she won't. She's incapable of love."

I tightened my hold to the banister, feeling suddenly as though I were standing at the edge of a cliff. And then I heard it, what would have broken my heart had I let it.

"She's just a colleague, Mom, okay? A colleague. That's all she is."

WHEN HE CAME UPSTAIRS I WAS LYING IN BED WITH MY EYES SHUT, pretending to be asleep. The door creaked and closed again and I thought he might have walked back out of the room, but then I felt him moving toward me, settling down next to me, caving in the mattress with his weight, his hand on my back. For a long time he just sat there. Then he stood up and left, and by the time he returned I must have really been asleep, because I never felt him come in, or lie down next to me. I never felt him cover me with the blanket under which we awoke the next morning, or open the window to let the air in.

After serving us coffee and toaster waffles, Rose saw us to the driveway, where Robert sat parked in a convertible car, waiting for us. She handed me a plastic bag with the egg salad sandwiches she'd prepared for our train ride back to the city, wrapped in thick aluminum foil, and stood in her bathrobe and slippers on the dewy lawn, holding the robe closed with one arm while we got inside the car.

In the kitchen she'd kissed me goodbye and said that she hoped to see me at her Thanksgiving table. Now she stood waving her pale hand at me with clinical detachment, as though she had no specific plans to ever see me again and knew something about me I didn't.

As the car pulled out of the driveway I looked at her closely, and saw in her sorry smile and discerning eyes the mirror she'd been holding up to me all along.

CHAPTER 21

THE TOWN OF LIVINGSTON WITH ITS WHITE clock tower and periwinkle sky had flashed past our train car, crowded with rush-hour passengers heading into the city, when I turned from the window and met Aeden's eyes.

"What's wrong?" Aeden asked me. The newspaper we'd gotten at the station was still folded on his lap.

"Nothing's wrong," I said, not knowing where to start.

"I'm going to Cambridge next week," he said. "For the interview. I was thinking if you came with me we could spend some time in Boston. It would be nice to get away for a few days, just the two of us."

I wanted to sweep things under the rug, but I knew I couldn't. "I don't know if that's a good idea, Aeden."

I could feel him studying me from his seat. "Why wouldn't it be?" he asked.

"I'm incapable of love," I answered, despite myself.

There was a stirring from one of the passengers in our booth, followed by the empty silence of before. Aeden unfolded the newspaper, as if to read it, and then he just sat there, looking stunned.

For the duration of the ride he did not speak to me again, or even look at me. I saw him gazing with stony interest at the *BMC Bioinformatics* pointlessly anchored in my hands and wished I could take my words back, and then I also wondered if there was any point in wishing this.

The line of people waiting outside Penn Station for a taxi reached the end of the block. We crossed Seventh Avenue and be-gan to head north on foot, moving awkwardly between swarms of morning commuters. The chive and egg salad sandwiches Rose had prepared were in my backpack. I'd had a vision of us stopping at his dorm to have them before heading to the Animal Facility to check on our mice, but my statement on the train had probably made that idea unlikely.

So I was surprised when, some five minutes later, beneath a giant billboard running a perfume ad in Times Square, Ae-den took hold of my hand and guided me to the inner side of the street. "I don't share my mother's views, Emily. I'm sorry you overheard what you did, and I apologize for saying what I said. You know that's not how I feel about you. You're not just a col-league to me."

"That doesn't change who I am, Aeden."

"There's nothing wrong with who you are."

Something told me to leave it at that, but I found myself telling him what I'd been thinking since that overheard conversation. "I don't know that I want the same things you want, Aeden, or that I would be able to manage them, even if I did. I know I told you the other day that I wanted to have children. The truth is, I don't know where that came from, if it was me who said it or a wishful version of me."

"It was you," Aeden said with a smile. "I was there."

"I don't want to mislead you anymore," I said.

"What does that mean?"

"It's not fair to you, Aeden, or to me."

Aeden dug into his backpack for a cigarette. I don't know what I was expecting him to say, but when he finally looked at me again, I wasn't prepared for his question. "So you want us to break up?"

For a painful moment I stood there speechless. Then I turned from him and dove into the crowded street, and began to walk away quickly, mindlessly weaving my way in my dress and heels between a million people, and then gradually slowing down, finding an empty pocket in the herd to catch my breath.

I can't remember what my precise thoughts were as I made my lonely advance toward the lab that morning. I only recall a powerful wish to turn the clock back to before our visit to Livingston. And yet along with this there was something else: a deep, almost visceral sense of peace I sometimes have riding those long moving walkways at airport terminals. Gradually I come to terms with the monotone motion of the rolling belt, the sight of people breezing by with their carry-ons and their smartphones, content-looking people who seem to have no regrets in the world, so that by the time the belt rolls to its end I'm usually reluctant to step off, and wish I could stay on for a little longer, pretend I'm one of them.

Somewhere farther uptown, between Lexington and Park, the sea-breeze scent of Aeden seized me like a blow to the stomach. I turned my head around, hoping to see him behind me, but moving toward me were only the faces of strangers.

CHAPTER 22

A MONG MY LIST OF EMAILS THAT MORNING WAS one from Justin, and I was pleased to see that unlike the others I had received from him since the Sunday he'd seen Aeden and me coming out of the darkroom together, this one was private: a reply to a message I had sent him some three months earlier telling him about our chimera in the facility, and how we hoped to have results before the end of fall. When I opened his email, however, there was no reply to my message of that day, only a link to a document. I opened the link and read *Novel Gene Mediates Axon Pathfinding in Drosophila,* and for a long time I just sat there at my desk, unable to read anything beyond that title, or even to think.

It was Craig's paper, of course, submitted to *Science* and fallen by some strange glitch of fate into Justin's hands for review. Justin would no doubt find a million little faults with it and anonymously ask for more data or even for additional experiments to be carried out in order to delay their publication, but there was only so much he could do.

I picked up the landline in our bay and dialed Aeden's cell phone, but there was no answer. I hit Redial and the call went straight to voicemail, and when I tried to leave him a message his mailbox was full. Noon came around and I hadn't heard from him. I sat with two printed copies of the paper on my lap and dialed him again and again and still there was no answer. By late afternoon I had brought myself to look at the paper closely enough to know that the gene Craig had discovered in his mutant flies was a close relative of our pathfinder. This meant that, from a purely scientific standpoint, the San Diego lab had reached the finish line before we had. One image in particular sent my heart racing: green fluorescent nerve endings in a small cross section of a fly antennal lobe unraveled from one another like telephone wires in a pole after a tornado, failing to reach their target. Coming across the image again, as I did years later—in the journal where Craig eventually published his results—I still found it hard to tear myself away from it.

I was about to stand up and go across the street to look for Aeden when Justin came into our bay escorted by David. Instinctively I glanced toward the window. The day outside had slipped by. The sky was ashen, the bridge a lifeless frame beneath it.

"You need to analyze your mice," Justin said, standing next to my chair. It was his first time in our bay since that Sunday, his first time addressing me. He was dressed formally as usual, and oozing from his mouth was a reassuring smell of wintergreen.

"That's not possible," I said. "The litter is only three days old."

"It can be done," Justin said. "We can learn something from these animals."

"Their map of smell isn't fully developed."

"That's Aeden talking," Justin said in a friendly tone. "Not you."

"How can we learn anything without the whole picture?" I asked, ignoring his comment.

"That depends on the results," Justin said. "If they're clear-cut we'll see it right away. Come morning, or later tonight, after my dinner engagement, I'll start working on the paper. By the end of the week we'll submit a Letters article to *Nature* describing our findings. Top-tier journals love competition, and what better competition than *Science* versus *Nature*?"

I remember wanting to get the analyses over and done with, to know the result of our experiment once and for all. "Aeden isn't here," I said. "We'll need to wait for him."

"David is here," Justin offered. "You can fetch the litter with him. He'll dissect the mice for you and stain the bulbs. He's done it before, haven't you, David?"

David gave me a sheepish look from my bench, where he'd been hanging out with an empty mouse cart, listening to our conversation and looking all too eager to help.

"I can't analyze the mice without Aeden," I said. "He's an equal contributor."

"Some equal contributor," Justin snapped. "To disappear when you need him." He looked reproachfully at me. "I should never have allowed it."

"That wasn't for you to decide, Justin."

"It *was* for me to decide. I regret I ever raised a finger in his favor."

When Aeden showed up in the bay minutes later, wearing the same clothes as earlier in the day and smelling of cigarettes, I sprang from my chair and hurried to him with Craig's paper. He calmly took it from my hands and stood at his workbench, leafing through the pages, and stopped at the image of the misrouted neurons and smiled; a pensive smile that seemed to have less to do with the threat of Craig's findings than with the marvel that they exposed. "If I were a reviewer I would approve," he finally said.

"It's settled, then," Justin said from my desk. "We're analyzing the litter tonight."

Aeden raised his eyes from the paper and looked at me.

"It will give us a head start," I said.

"What head start?" Aeden said, turning to Justin. "When have we ever examined newborns?"

Justin smoothed the scalloped chain of the watch he'd been holding. "I don't care about protocol, Aeden—it's not the way to get ahead in this field. Not in this day and age. You of all people should know that."

Aeden shrugged. "I'm not going to sacrifice our only litter because of what may or may not happen with Craig's submission. That's insane."

Justin glanced at me for assistance. When I didn't give it to him he tucked his watch into his jeans and smiled at Aeden with composure. Then he slowly walked over to where Aeden and I were standing, the three of us forming a sort of triangle. "You'll have a new litter down the road, Aeden. Meanwhile you will do as I say."

Aeden stared away from him, toward the open door of the lab. I had a feeling he was about to leave the room, but he didn't. He looked at me, uneasily, and it came as a somewhat strange and magnificent surprise to hear him say, "All right, I'll see what I can do."

Justin pushed the empty cart at him. "Good."

———

ON THE THIRD FLOOR OF THE ANIMAL FACILITY THE HALLWAY lights drew glinting slats across the polished floor, like sun-

light reflected off an oil-spilled highway. On our way there Aeden and I had discussed Craig's paper: the green fluorescent
neurons wandering the antennal lobe of the fly like blind mi-
grants, never reaching their destination. Aeden had stared unblinkingly ahead, impressed by the findings and also strangely
aloof. We were approaching room 310 at the end of the hallway,
where our mice were housed, when he looked at me and asked,
"Are you sure this is what you want to do, Emily?"

"Yes," I answered, though I wasn't sure that it was what we
should do.

We parked the mouse cart outside the room, unlocked the
door, and stepped inside. I held a hand in front of me as my eyes
adjusted to the darkness, until I could make out the rows of plastic cages, aligned on metal racks from floor to ceiling, and the
mice, crawling like sleepwalkers.

What stood out, and never had before, were the white cards
hanging from the front of each cage, with the names of the
mouse strains clearly printed. These were the cards Aeden had
mentioned, the cards Craig had switched around before fleeing
the lab, leaving the investigators with mice in the room months
behind in their experiments.

A blinding light pierced the darkness: the biosafety hood at
the end of the room. Aeden had switched on the lights and moved
to a nearby rack, where he stood examining a row of unfamiliar cages. The cage with our litter was already inside the hood:
the sash was raised and I could see the female knockout founder
crouched beside the water spigot, next to her mound of pups. I
went to stand in front of the hood and her whiskers twitched in
my direction, as if smelling me.

Aeden lifted a cage from the row he'd been looking at and

carried it over to the hood. It was only when he settled the cage down alongside ours, and I saw the newborn litter inside it, that it hit me that something was wrong. Before I could process his intentions, Aeden swapped the cage labels so that the card in the metal holder of our cage no longer read APELL AND DOHERTY, but DOHERTY AND MELTZER.

"What are you doing, Aeden?" I asked.

He switched the hood lights back off. In the darkness I could see him moving away from me, with one cage in each hand. He carried them over to the rack he'd been standing next to and slid them into transposed slots, matching their fake labels. "If Justin sends David out here to look for them he'll take the wrong mice." He rolled the rack back against the wall and started toward the door, empty-handed.

"This is unheard of." I wheeled the rack away from the wall and pulled out our mislabeled cage. Something caught my foot and I tripped, nearly letting go of the cage. Holding on to it, I staggered toward the door to find Aeden standing against it, blocking my way out. He was gazing at me in a tired way, as if my intentions were absurd.

"If you take them out you'll never be able to return them," he said.

"You agreed to analyze them, Aeden."

He shook his head. "I never said I would."

"I won't let you do this."

"What won't you let me do, Emily, save our only litter from the pompous asshole who calls himself a lab head? Look, I've never done something like this, but I'm doing it now for your sake."

I shut my eyes.

"You can sacrifice them if you want," Aeden continued. "If

you're so desperate to analyze them, I won't stop you, but I'll let you in on a secret—if the results are unclear, we won't be able to publish them. Not only that, but we will have to cross the founders again and wait for the next litter, and that could take months."

Outside, along the path of elms leading from the Animal Facility to our research building, rain pattered on our heads, and on the empty cart in front of us. We deposited the cart in the lab and walked back out. It was close to midnight and no one was around, not even David. The hallway was weakly lit, the air depressingly heavy with the self-scheming drone of machines. On the drizzling sidewalk to our dorms I found myself walking several steps ahead of Aeden, refusing the cover of his umbrella and shaking my wet hair at his suggestion that we pick up our conversation of earlier, the one we'd left unfinished in the street.

I slept in my own bed that night, and the night after that, and it was a while before I was able to talk to Aeden; a while before I was able to shake off the feeling that in not analyzing our mice, in returning the cage to the rack with my own two hands, something had been irredeemably altered. Steered off track, like those neurons in Craig's paper.

———————

A WEEK LATER WE WERE IN ROOM 310 AGAIN, CHECKING ON OUR litter, when Aeden broke the news to me. "I have a job offer," he said. He'd gone to Cambridge for the interview and returned the next day looking triumphant.

A loud air was circulating inside the hood, and I pretended not to hear him. In the hoods it was possible to do that. Words got lost in the windswept air all the time. But he knew I'd heard. "Aren't you going to say anything?" he asked.

"Congratulations," I offered.

One of the pups from the litter roamed the palm of his hand, eyes shut, tail between his legs, his fur shining in the light like tree bark. Within a week they had grown coats. Another three weeks and they would be old enough to analyze. *Three weeks*, I thought. In only three weeks we would have results, and if they were positive I believed Aeden would decide to stay in the lab.

He released the chirping mouse back inside the cage and covered it with the grid and the plastic lid. The card on the metal holder now read APELL AND DOHERTY. Justin had sent me an email threatening to analyze the pups himself, but the litter of mice in the cage with our name was untouched after ten days, so we'd swapped back the labels.

"Nothing too fancy," Aeden said. "Space is a little tight and resources are limited but at least I'll be able to choose what to work on, as long as it has to do with neuron growth and regeneration. I'll also have an experienced technician at hand, and a real salary, for the first time in my life. Not a bad package?"

"Decent," I said, though I hadn't intended to say this, or anything else about Neurogen.

"I hope more than just decent. I said yes to them."

I looked at him then. "You said yes?"

"I've been wanting to talk to you about it, Emily, but you keep avoiding the subject."

I was no longer standing with him at the hood, but moving away. Somewhere between his mention of Neurogen and the realization that he was seriously intent on leaving, I'd unconsciously started walking toward the door.

"Is it so terrible of me to want out?" Aeden asked behind me.

"No. I think it's great," I answered, hurrying out of the room.

He followed me outside. "You don't really mean that."

"I do," I said. "I think it's very wise of you to want to give up on the project and everything you've been working toward for the last four years of your life to go bury yourself in some obscure start-up company in the middle of nowhere."

"What would you like me to do?" Aeden said, catching up to me. "Stay in the asshole's lab forever?"

"Stop calling him that," I said angrily. "Whoever Justin is, he deserves to be treated with respect."

It was early in the morning, the time of day when there are more workers in an animal facility than there are investigators. I couldn't see them, the men in scrubs and face masks who tended to the needs of the thousands of mice on our floor: I could only make out the music they listened to in the inner hallway running parallel to the one Aeden and I were moving through, and it may as well have been music from another planet, it felt so foreign.

I had nearly reached the exit door when Aeden stepped ahead of me, in front of the silver handle. I turned from the door, with the idea of running to the elevators at the end of the floor, but he caught hold of my arm. "What do you want me to do, Emily?"

"Clearly it doesn't matter what I want," I said, pulling my arm from his grasp. "You've already made plans for yourself."

"Come with me."

"What?"

"It doesn't have to be Neurogen, or even Cambridge," Aeden said. "I'll go anywhere else, as long as we're together."

For a moment I thought he wasn't serious, but he was. There was something almost humbling in his smile, something that made me realize he'd been turning over the idea in his head for a while.

"I'm not leaving the lab, Aeden." What I told him next surprised me, and it also didn't. "I will never abandon this project."

A look of hurt rushed to his face and lingered on for several moments, and then he was gone. Before I could retract my words he'd swung the door open and walked out into the staircase and I was alone in the hallway. I tried to picture myself opening the door and running after him down the stairs, but couldn't. So I remained where I was, staring at the place where Aeden had stood and listening to his footsteps recede, until the only sound that I could hear, like a distant heart murmur, was that of the music on the floor.

CHAPTER 23

Aeden began spending more time at his desk, surfing the Neurogen website and reading every paper on neuron growth and regeneration he could get his hands on. He spoke to me only when necessary, and when he looked at me from his desk, or while we made our way along the path of elms to the Animal Facility, there was always a question in his eyes, and it seemed to have little to do with the project or the mice or whatever it was I was inevitably talking about, and everything to do with what I had told him that morning.

More and more often I found myself alone with my thoughts on the terrace of our dorm building, where old-timers in the university—among them Aeden—had watched the Twin Towers crumble. On the bleakest of days, with the southernmost tip of the island a gray spot in the distance, the chimera often came to mind. Not the spotted male on whose progeny the experiment hinged, but what Rose, with her discerning eyes, had said about unrealizable dreams.

I kept dwelling on it—what she had told me—because of how I felt, knowing that Aeden would be leaving the lab after we analyzed the litter, but mainly because of what happened a few days later, after that morning, and could have been avoided had he and I been together as a couple.

I already mentioned that in the spring of that year, around the time Aeden and I began working in the tissue culture room, a new graduate student from Boston by the name of Ginny Wu came to work in the lab, and that she was given what had formerly been my bay in the main room, and wore too much perfume.

Since those days in the tissue culture room, half a year had passed, and in all those months neither Aeden nor I had ever approached or said to Ginny more than what people working in the same lab usually say to each other: *how's it going, it's muggy out there, I saw a package for you in the cold room, the lecture is about to start, have a good night, you too.*

I had often seen her in the conference room, having lunch with the other graduate students, and after lunch, after everyone had gone back to work, sitting alone at the table skimming the *New York Times* with her willowy fingers and a downcast, self-conscious sort of smile. I'm saying this because, as I remember it, six months had gone by and I'd hardly ever seen her working. In the beginning, her first month or two in the lab, she could be seen following David around in a lab coat, learning the ropes from him and ambling into people's bays with a notepad and pen, but as the months progressed she seemed to have stopped trying. More often than not I saw her sitting idle in the conference room, or sneaking out of the lab before sundown with the robin's-egg-blue case in which I imagined her oboe lay nestled, wrapped in layers of felt.

It took me a while to realize that the reason Ginny hadn't really started working on anything didn't have to do with laziness or indifference, but with her inability to find a promising research project in a lab where such projects were already taken. With time it became obvious to me that she had no special skills, nothing that would have enabled her to carve out a niche for herself, and that Justin had probably taken her in on the basis of some glowing recommendation and because she was a Harvard graduate who spoke Mandarin fluently and played for a small and well-regarded chamber ensemble that gave benefit concerts throughout the city, including at the lecture hall at AUSR.

That is how I saw her situation, and from the little I came to learn about her, my impressions were more or less accurate. Being her senior in the lab, and sensing how lost she was, I supposed that I could have made more of an effort to be nice to her, taken her under my wing and found something for her to do while she figured things out for herself. But I was caught up with the project, and there was also what Aeden had told me about the guys in the lab liking Ginny, and my supposition that he did too, whether or not he would admit to it. And also, though I hated to acknowledge it, I felt threatened by her and didn't want to feel more ridiculous and mean-spirited about it than I already did. So I never offered to help.

But then neither did Aeden. As a general rule we kept our distance from her, and I would probably have little or no recollection of Ginny today had it not been for all the scientific discussions her perfume inspired between Aeden and me. But also, had she not walked into our bay one morning during this period when Aeden and I were not really talking.

We had returned from room 310, and I was anxious to get back to work on a human gene I'd recently come across, in a new DNA database, whose sequence bore a faint resemblance to that of the pathfinder gene. I remember my screen lit up with the sequence at the same time that I registered a disturbing smell, and I looked up to find Ginny standing there in front of me with her notepad and pen.

She made to smile, but probably seeing that I wasn't about to do the same, quickly aborted the effort. "I'm sorry to bother you."

"It's no bother at all," I said flatly. She was wearing an interesting sweater, tissue white with a bright yellow lemon in the middle. It looked like a still life painting.

"Justin told me you knocked out a gene. I'd appreciate it if you could give me some pointers about the procedure."

I was surprised she hadn't gone straight to Aeden with the request, and then realized Justin had probably neglected to tell her who had engineered the mutation. I glanced at Aeden, but he hadn't looked away from his screen, and I assumed he had no interest in helping Ginny either. "Do you mind if we talk later?" I said, not giving her a specific time or place.

"Not a problem," Ginny said, and with a cheerful smile she trailed off, out of our bay and back into hers.

"You could have been more forthcoming, Emily," Aeden said behind me, as soon as Ginny was gone. "The poor girl doesn't know where she's standing."

I wanted to let the matter die, but for some reason didn't. "So could you, Aeden. You're the expert here, after all, not me."

And that is how it all began.

Later that afternoon, on my way to the restroom, I saw them in the conference room. Ginny's notepad was open on the table and she held her pen in her hand, but she wasn't taking notes. She was nodding at Aeden, slowly, with a reined-in sort of enthusiasm that led me to understand they weren't discussing science. I wondered who had sought out whom, and told myself it didn't matter; soon enough Aeden would be done talking to her.

I had returned to my desk when Ginny walked hurriedly past me and disappeared into her bay, emerging shortly thereafter with her blue leather case. Not more than a minute passed before a nasal sound emerged from the depths of the hallway, raspy and broken at first and then increasingly fluid, gathering momentum and flooding every nook and cranny of the room with a magnanimous warmth so alien to the lab it was impossible to ignore.

Within moments the entire lab had flocked to the conference room, including Justin, who rarely left his office for anything. From where I stood I could see the bronze tail end of Ginny's oboe, and her fingers moving up and down, and I could see Aeden. He was sitting at the edge of his seat, with his back to the whiteboard, and the arresting smile in his eyes as he watched her play struck a deep, sad chord in me.

After an interminable eight minutes or so, Ginny lowered her oboe and curtsyed, a genuine bow, and smiled with a sleepy face as if she were stepping out of a dream and only just noticing us. In the midst of all the commotion and applause I heard Aeden ask her what she'd played, but her answer was lost to me across the sultry air.

CHAPTER 24

F OR A WHILE, AFTER THAT AFTERNOON, I WILLED
myself not to think about Ginny. People didn't
just strike up a friendship after their first conversation, but as
the days passed and I saw Aeden with her more often, it felt almost inevitable that they had. I caught a glimpse of them in the
cafeteria one day, conversing at a corner table over their trays of
food, and I began to bring sandwiches from home again. I knew
that Aeden wasn't with her in that way, that he wasn't seriously
involved with Ginny, and yet I couldn't help but ask myself what
this unlikely and unforeseen relationship between them was
based on: their love of music, the novelty of their diverse back-
grounds, the fact that Aeden was able to easily provide the help
and guidance she obviously needed in the lab?

The days Ginny left the lab early with her instrument case,
Aeden walked her dog—an old bloodhound with sad brown eyes
whose existence I'd previously been unaware of. A smell of earth
would come rolling like moist vapor through the open door of the
lab, and before I could blink the dog would be standing in front
of me with a yellow tennis ball clutched in his mouth, Aeden
trailing behind with the leash.

For some reason the dog always came straight to me. Trembling, he would drop the ball into my hand and fix his brown eyes on mine with nostalgia, as if on the lookout for something. "Hi there," I'd say, patting the soft crown of his head, and the dog would start to whine.

"Cut it out, Smokey," Aeden would say to him. And what inevitably brought a smile to my face: "Can't you see people are trying to work around here?"

The dog would shoot him an uncomprehending look and slump down on the floor, next to me, and there he would remain, blowing hot air onto my legs until Aeden finished doing whatever he'd come to the lab to do, which short of checking his emails or clicking icons on the Neurogen website was nothing. His late afternoon visits to the main room with Smokey clearly had something to do with me, and though we were hardly on speaking terms at this point, they were still somehow good moments. The only worthwhile moments I recall of that period in the lab, leading up to the analysis of our mice.

It was during one of those lazy afternoons, sitting back-to-back at our desks, the dog curled at my feet, that Aeden brought up the idea of taking the project with me. I'd been unduly examining the sequence alignment on my screen, searching for homologues of the pathfinder gene, when I heard him swivel his chair around, and felt his eyes on me. I didn't turn around, but he said, "Nothing is going on between Ginny and me, Emily. I realize you probably find that hard to believe, but it's the truth. She and I are just friends."

"I'm relieved to hear that," I said. "I wouldn't want you to be bored out of your mind, though I'm sure your mother would approve of Ginny."

Aeden was sniffling behind me—his way of laughing when I was being ironic. Then he said, "You wouldn't have to abandon the project, Emily. You could take it with you to another lab, maybe even your own, and you could build your own DNA database, and keep searching for gene relatives. After we analyze the mice and the paper is written, nothing forces you to stay here anymore."

"Justin would never allow it," I said. "You know how he is, he'll do everything in his power to stop me from taking the project from his lab. Just as he's probably doing everything to delay Craig's publication."

"There's nothing he can do to stop you," Aeden said. "Once the paper is written you're free to leave. We could leave together."

I sat gazing at the alignment on my screen. What he was proposing I do was reasonable, maybe even doable, but that wasn't what troubled me. "It's not just the project, Aeden," I finally said. "It's mostly about what I told you the other day, which you didn't want to hear." After another pause I added, "I'm not sure that I'm the right person for you."

"I'm not asking you to marry me, Emily." I turned from my screen to look at him, and saw in his face the stubborn determination his voice had not conveyed. "Promise me you'll think about it."

"I will," I said, knowing that I would. "I'll think about it." I stood from my chair and picked up my handbag.

"Where are you going?"

"Home," I said, trying to sound casual about it. What I needed was to be alone, to assimilate what he'd said.

"I'll phone you tonight."

"I'll need a little more time," I said.

And then, without looking back, I hurried across the hallway, feeling a surprising burst of joy inside me, the dog whimpering anxiously behind me. "Go back, Smokey," I said, suspecting he would try to follow me all the way to the elevator. "Go back."

CHAPTER 25

I WALKED INTO OUR BAY EARLY THE NEXT MORNING expecting to find Aeden sitting where I'd left him the previous day, and was disappointed to discover that he wasn't. I hung my handbag on the armrest of my chair, gathered the ear puncher and surgical scissors and a fresh batch of Eppendorf tubes from Aeden's workbench, and sat down to wait for him. We were scheduled to genotype our litter of mice in the facility.

The room, I remember, was ominously quiet—that first half of the morning when experiments are underway and time feels suspended. For a while I gazed distractedly out the window, wondering if Aeden had forgotten we were supposed to meet early and whether I should phone him to remind him, when I spotted Smokey scuttling unleashed on the overpass below, and Aeden and Ginny a little ways behind him. The sun was beating down on them, and being several stories above them as I was I could barely make out his face, but what struck me as all too real, to the point of feeling obvious, was that he and she and the dog looked almost like a family. As I watched them, Ginny bent down to scrape dog shit from the sun-warped pavement, wearing jeans that were too tight on her, and Aeden smoked a cigarette and dragged his feet lethargically, and yet they seemed to be together in some casual, nonaccidental way. Together in that spontaneous fluid way in which the kids from Shaw Woods had been together. Together in a way I feared Aeden and I would never be together even if it were just the two of us alone, stranded on Mars for the rest of our lives.

——————

JUSTIN, WHEN I SHOWED UP IN HIS OFFICE MOMENTS LATER, FEELing miserable and bent out of shape after seeing Aeden and Ginny together, was rearranging travel mementos on his walnut bookcase. He turned from the bookcase to look at me, and I could tell that he was pleased to see me there, in his private quarters for the first time in months. He had ignored the emails I had sent him explaining the scientific reasoning behind my decision to postpone the analysis of the litter, and I hadn't summoned the courage or the nerve to explain myself in person. My decision to wait for the mice to be older had been heavily influenced by Aeden, and he knew it.

Now he deposited the broken-looking object in his hands back on the shelf. "What can I do for you, Emily?"

On my way there I'd made a mental note to ask him about the status of Craig's paper, and knew before even stepping into his office that I wouldn't, that the moment I came face-to-face with Justin, the question I had never dared to ask him, and had wanted to ever since my return from Livingston, would come pouring out of me. "You once told me," I began, in as steady a voice as I could produce, "you said that I reminded you of yourself, at my age. You mentioned ambition, single-mindedness, loneliness, but these are just a few of the things that we have in common, aren't they?"

Justin motioned with his head toward the puddle of light bathing his makeshift living room. I went to settle on my usual spot on the couch, and he on his wing-backed chair, diagonally facing me. I glanced at the window, too self-conscious to look at him after what I'd brought myself to ask.

"You obviously don't know what it's like to be me, Justin," I said. "You're not in my head to know it. But that day, when I expressed my concern for Aeden and you called me insane, it felt like you were trying to warn me about something."

Justin smiled at me, for the first time in months. A knowing smile I felt I could trust, despite my history with him. "People like you and me," he said, "we're made of a different fabric than most people. A name doesn't do justice to the fine genetic differences between individuals, except maybe to help you confirm what you already know, or suspect. We're not built like everyone else. We're not meant to be with other people in the way in which they're with each other. Does this make sense to you?"

It did, but not completely. "What about love?" I asked.

"Love?" Justin said, chuckling. "You might find it, but it won't last very long. We may feel desperately alone, but deep down what we crave is solitude. Your best bet is here, academia. This is where you stand the best chance of being happy, and making others happy." He looked at me and paused. "If I'm upsetting you I'll stop."

I looked away from him. "It's just your opinion," I said. "Besides, we're not identical, you and I."

"You came here to ask for my opinion, didn't you?"

"I wish I hadn't."

"If it's any consolation, Emily, everyone in this world is alone. We're all sentenced to solitary confinement inside our own skins."

I smiled, looking at him again. "You stole that from some-where."

"Tennessee Williams," Justin admitted, with a sad little snort. "First editions of his works." He pointed to the scattered spines on the lower shelf of his bookcase, level with the floor. "Would you like to read them?"

I didn't. The quote was enough. The quote, I knew, would suffice for a lifetime.

An hour passed, or it might have been seconds, before I had the presence of mind to stand up. For what felt like an eternity I sat there with a finger pressed to my temple, gazing beyond his shoulder at the blown-up olfactory bulb above his desk, seeing it not for what it was, but for what it might appear to be to an outside observer: an atlas of the world with distinct aerial routes unwaveringly charted between cities and countries and islands in the ocean. I wanted to ask him if he ever got lonely being up in the sky in his Piper, with no one around to share the view. But I doubt that I ever asked the question, because I would probably remember the answer today if I had, and I don't.

I had stood up from the couch and nearly reached the door when Justin said, "I know why you're here, Emily. I got a call from Neurogen last month, someone from management inquiring about Aeden."

"I hope you were generous," I said.

"Exceedingly. I have no interest in keeping him here, as you can imagine. He's too autonomous for his own good, and a bad influence on you. I'm glad you're not with him anymore. I see him outside often, with the new girl, Ginny. That must have been a blow to you, but it's better that way, believe me."

When I turned around to look at him, Justin was stretched out in his chair, yawning. "Aeden wants me to go with him," I said. "After the paper is written."

Justin made to readjust his glasses over the bridge of his nose, but didn't. Instead he smiled at me, as if the revelation had offset the need for a better view. "Have you packed your bags yet?"

"Don't be ridiculous," I said, and knowing I had said too much, added, "Please forget we ever had this conversation."

"Which part?"

"This last part, obviously."

Justin winced away from me, toward the sun creeping through the slats of his window. "I already forgot," he said.

BUT HE DIDN'T. TWO DAYS LATER, ON A LATE NIGHT LIKE ANY other night in the lab, a night I probably would only vaguely recall today had it not been for what happened, Justin sauntered past Aeden, who was loading DNA samples from the tails of our mice into the gel on his workbench, and plopped down next to me, onto Aeden's vacant desk chair. He was wearing a pinstripe suit with a bow tie, and his shoes smelled heavily of polish, which made me suspect he was on his way out to some formal gathering with university patrons instead of the blind date he would probably have preferred. He stretched his legs out, in Aeden's direction. "Working late?"

Aeden shrugged. "It depends what you mean by late." He went on ejecting the blue samples into the wells of the gel, giving no sign of reading anything between the lines.

The conversation I'd had with Justin two days earlier came flooding back to me, accompanied by a feeling of imminent disaster. "To what do we owe your visit?" I asked, in a lowered voice.

Justin turned casually toward me. Until then, his focus had been on Aeden. "The San Diego lab retracted their submission."

"That's excellent news," I said, warily.

"Yes and no. They could be planning to add new findings to their paper, or maybe they were unable to reproduce their results, in which case the role of your gene would fall into doubt. But regardless of the reason for their retraction, a change of plan is in order. I'm going to withhold publication of the knockout data. What we want now is a larger paper, one that will include sequence information for closely related genes. It's only a matter of time before you or someone else in the lab finds them, Emily."

"I don't understand," I said. "What do you mean someone else?"

"You told me just the other day you were thinking of leaving this lab. You're free to leave now," Justin said.

Aeden, who'd stopped pipetting, gazed inquiringly at me from his bench. Since my visit to Justin I'd avoided the topic of our leaving together. I looked away from him, back at Justin. "I didn't say I wanted to leave the lab. That's not what I said."

"Maybe those weren't your exact words," Justin said, examining his cuticles. "But the implication was clear."

"This is unnecessary, Justin. I have no plans to leave, and you know it."

"That's not what it sounded like when we last spoke," he said.

Aimlessly I asked, "Why are you doing this?"

Justin smiled at me. "I'm doing nothing wrong, Emily, aside from giving you the option to leave. I wouldn't want you to stay here against your will, just because you feel obliged to finish your appointment. The project will go on without you."

"I'm not staying here against my will, Justin." The more I

tried to reason with him, the more I felt as though I were digging my own grave, yet I couldn't bring myself to stop. "I want to stay in this lab."

"Really?" Justin said. "You could have certainly fooled me."

"That's not true," I said. I remember stealing a look at Aeden and thinking, in my muddled state, that the building was about to collapse. "You're making things up, Justin."

"You told me Aeden wanted you to leave with him after the paper was written. Weren't those your exact words? Well, I'm afraid that option is no longer available to you, Emily, but the option to leave is."

I was suddenly staring down at his shoes, in which the ceiling lights were reflected. "I'm not leaving," I said faintly.

"You came to me the other day with a problem," Justin continued. "I'm offering you a solution."

"But I'm not leaving." My voice was breaking now. "I'm not going with him."

"*Emily!*" It was Aeden. I glanced up and for a moment locked eyes with him, feeling a weight on my chest. "I'm sorry," I murmured.

Justin swiveled his chair back toward him. "What about you, Aeden?" His tone was almost jovial. "Any objections about the future of this project?"

Aeden's gaze had fallen on the window of our bay. He shook his head, as if he didn't care one way or another, but I could see something dark and worrying mounting behind his eyes.

"I hope you realize what this means, Aeden," Justin added. "You will no longer be an equal contributor in Emily's paper, if there is one. Not that you need that little star attached to your surname anymore, with your new job in industry."

Aeden said nothing to this, or maybe he mumbled a word or two or three. The truth is I don't know: Like the victim of an accident is unable to remember those pivotal seconds before the blow, so am I, or maybe I've willed myself to forget them so as not to carry that moment around with me for the rest of my life. I don't know.

What I can remember is the multichannel pipette ominously balanced at the edge of Aeden's workbench, threatening to fall and crash to the floor, and a second later the scent of shoe polish unraveled in the air to a toxic turpentine odor. By the time Aeden reached the chair where Justin was sitting Justin had sprung to his feet, but too late. I jumped out of my chair between them and saw a fist flying toward me.

The punch came so assuredly I imagined Aeden delicately pushing my face out of the way, when in fact the heel of his hand had gone straight into my nose. There was no sound, not even pain, only a pounding reverberation in my skull. I cupped my nose between my hands and fell back onto my chair. Something warm and metallic was in my mouth, and it was the taste of my own blood.

When I opened my eyes Aeden and I were alone in the room, and he was kneeling beside me with a bag of crushed ice.

"Is my nose broken?" I asked.

"Swollen," he said.

For some reason I asked, "Will it be broken?"

He brushed off the question with a smile, but his eyes were moist and angered in a way I can't quite begin to describe even today, after eleven years.

"You should have seen the look on his face," I said—though I hadn't seen Justin's face—and, making an effort to laugh, added, "It was like a truck was coming at him."

Aeden wasn't humored. He kept holding the ice bag to my philtrum, that delicate space between nose and mouth, looking like he was about to weep. I heard the clock on the wall ticking and wondered what it would be like to stand up and leave with him and never return to the lab. And I knew that I wouldn't do that.

"You can't stay here anymore," he said.

"Yes, I can," I said. "This is where I belong."

CHAPTER 26

WE ANALYZED THE MICE THE NEXT DAY. I remember, before going into the lab that morning, standing in jeans and a turtleneck sweater by the window of my dorm, nursing a mug of coffee—black coffee, because the milk in my refrigerator smelled rotten. Sunlight was streaming across the glass of the window, and the rays felt like tiny daggers in my eyes. I had slept poorly, a shallow sleep without dreams, but then I'd hardly been sleeping at all for the last three weeks.

By eight A.M. Aeden and I had gone into room 310 to retrieve our knockout litter. The four-week-old mice, technically adults, were huddled in a corner of the cage, over a pale white mountain of bedding. Some of them were asleep and some weren't, and those that were awake seemed to be staring straight at us, but of course they weren't. Mice don't make eye contact. Unlike humans, they rely mainly on smell to navigate the world.

By nine A.M. Aeden had sacrificed and dissected the six homozygous knockout animals in the litter. They'd gone down quietly, without a squeal, as mice often do when handled expertly, and now their heads, reduced to dinosaur-shaped little skulls with

hollowed eye sockets and bulging olfactory bulbs, were swaying inside glass vials on a rocker on my bench. Aeden and I sat
on stools in front of the bench, saying little to each other. I kept
staring down at the timer in my hand, wanting the thirty-minute
neuron-staining incubation period to be over once and for all.
I was nervous and exhausted and I was pretty certain that Aeden felt the same way. His sweater reeked of cigarette, and he'd
uncharacteristically dropped his scalpel while dissecting one of
the animals. I asked him about his timer, which he usually wore
clipped to his sweater, and for an instant, before telling me he'd
lost it, Aeden seemed not to know what I was talking about.

When the half hour was nearly over, before my timer started
beeping, Aeden lifted one of the vials off the rocker and held it
up to the light. Through the clear walls of the vial I could see a
pair of olfactory bulbs floating in the yellow staining medium,
and faintly, very faintly, tiny specks of blue coating the curva-
ture of their surface, as if some invisible hand had dotted them
with a fine ballpoint pen. The olfactory nerve endings seemed
to have converged onto myriad targets, as they would have in a
normal mouse. I felt something shift within me: I had been so
sure they would not. But then, the naked eye, I told myself, is
often unreliable.

Minutes later we had transported the six vials to the imaging
room across the hallway, a tiny airless cockpit of a room so im-
possibly cramped with equipment that I had a hard time locating
the row of stereoscopes by the wall. It was Aeden who examined
the bulbs first, quietly. He switched the stage lights on and held
a vial horizontally over the stage, adjusting the focus knob of the
instrument and twirling the vial carefully between his bent fingers. He set the vial aside and picked up a second one and held it

and twirled it as he had the first. After only a few seconds he set this vial aside too and picked up a third, and it must have been here that I took in, with a vertiginous feeling in my gut, that things were not as I'd hoped.

Aeden rolled back his chair and stood up. I sat down on the chair and pressed my eyes to the eyepiece. The tiny blue specks I had seen earlier, in the main room, appeared before me again, but large and defined, like islands seen from a low-flying airplane; each blue island a bundle of blue nerve endings arrived at their destined target and meeting point. The map of smell was normal.

I felt the warmth of a hand on my shoulder, and heard Aeden ask me quietly, "Are you all right?"

I shook my head and stood up from the chair, feeling like I was about to throw up. And then I actually did throw up; the first wave of nausea hit me as I ran down the hallway, so that by the time I reached the women's bathroom and locked myself in a stall, my lab coat and hands were caked in vomit. I hunched over the toilet seat and heaved up the leftovers of the coffee.

"Emily?" Aeden stood on the other side of the metal door behind me. I couldn't believe he'd followed me into the bathroom, in broad daylight. "Emily, can I come in?"

There was an unsettling ring of fear in his voice I remember wanting very badly to put at rest. "It's okay, Aeden," I said. "The milk in my coffee was probably bad, that's all. Nothing to worry about."

Back in the imaging room we took pictures of the bulbs, dozens of pictures covering every ventral and dorsal and medial and lateral aspect of their surface, and hundreds upon hundreds of olfactory axons and their targets. We returned the bulbs to their vials and deposited the vials on Aeden's shelf in the cold room, and for the rest of the day we sat side-by-side at my desk examining the blown-up images on my laptop, hoping to spot misrouted nerve endings in a sea of biological normalcy.

Sometime late in the afternoon Justin showed up in our bay. On my way to the bathroom I'd run into several people, among them David, who I guessed had already given Justin wind of the situation. Justin didn't bother to ask about what we'd found. Speaking from the foot of the bay he demanded a written report of the results, with images to back them. He also wanted the six pairs of bulbs preserved in formaldehyde for future reference, and the chimera and the founders in room 310 to be kept alive in the event that we decided to breed more knockouts. Aeden sat all the while with his eyes fixed on my screen, ignoring Justin even after he was done speaking. I remember the silence between them, and Justin observing Aeden from a distance, snubbed and yet refusing to leave.

At six P.M. I sat alone in my dorm, reexamining the pictures on my laptop. The building was so quiet I could hear trapped air wheezing back and forth across the hallway outside, and the elevators aimlessly wandering from floor to floor. People rarely returned from the labs before it was dark outside, and until then neither had I.

On the screen in front of me, slender blue filaments converged on their targets like family members on a home. What had guided them there? Not the protein encoded by my gene, certainly not that, but something else: another axon guidance molecule yet to be discovered, or another cue altogether, or a combination of both these things. The data spoke for itself, and according to it the pathfinder was not the gene I had hoped to find. There would be no paper, and in the long run no lab. There would be no future such as the future I had envisioned for myself.

Beyond the windowpane of my dorm, on the upper deck of the bridge, a resting line of vehicles brought a giant parking lot to mind. I thought of Aeden's mother falling down the stairs, how she would probably never again smell the juniper she'd grown in her front yard, and my heart went out to her in a way it rarely had for anyone I'd ever known.

When I looked at the window again I saw my face silhouetted against the glass, and the headlights of cars moving smoothly toward the east. Darkness had snuck up on me, without my noticing it. I went on sitting there, feeling too heavy and too defeated to move, and it must have been here, more or less, that I got that email from Aeden—an email without a subject or even a message. I opened it imagining it had something to do with the mice, but it didn't. When I clicked on the attachment what I saw was the image of a footbridge connecting two redbrick buildings over a narrow channel of water. In large bold letters, across the wooden slats of the bridge, Aeden had written: *Come With Me.*

―――――――――

WHEN HE RANG THE DOORBELL SOME TWO HOURS LATER I WAS IN the kitchen, scrubbing the refrigerator shelves with liquid Ajax. During the two hours preceding this moment, which I had known was bound to come, I had kept myself busy vacuuming and disinfecting the floors and purging the refrigerator of the spoiled milk and mealy apples I hadn't trashed or replenished for weeks.

The ring was followed by a succession of knocks. "Emily. I know you're there."

"It's late, Aeden," I called, not going to the door.

"How are you feeling?"

"I have a splitting headache." This was partially true—the smell of detergent was starting to give me a headache—but the larger truth was that I was terrified to see him, to look him in the eyes after his message. To speak to him through the door was cowardly, ungrateful even, but I couldn't open it.

"I'm sorry about the experiment," Aeden said. "I really am. I know how you're feeling."

"You don't know," I said. "People are always saying things like that, claiming to know what others are feeling, but the truth is no one knows."

"If anyone can empathize with what you're going through, it's me, Emily. But has it ever occurred to you, you may be destined for greater things than the Nobel Prize?"

I could hear him laughing. "You have a lousy sense of humor, Aeden."

"Did you get my email?"

"I did."

"And?"

"The answer is no, I can't go with you."

"Why not?"

I remember I was no longer in the kitchen but standing by the door, with a sponge in my hand. "My appointment in the lab hasn't ended," I said. "And I just renewed the lease on this dorm."

On the other side of the door Aeden said, "Those aren't even excuses, Emily. You could pick up and leave with me tomorrow if you wanted to. Please open the door."

"It would never work," I said.

"We'll make it work," Aeden said. "You'll see. We'll get our own place, a nice little house with a yard and a dog. I know you like dogs, and I swear I'll never mow the lawn. I'll let the grass grow wild like your father used to, and we'll have friends over for dinner once a month. I know you don't like company very much. I would have liked to have people over every night, but I'll settle for once a month. We'll also have kids. Eventually. Two kids, like you said, or maybe just one. One should be enough."

"You're crazy," I said, but I could feel the smile on my face.

"I want to make you happy."

"What makes you think I'm not?" I asked.

I wasn't expecting him to answer, but he did. "You're too alone to be happy."

"Maybe it's in my nature to be alone," I said. "Maybe I'm destined to go through life alone, like those wandering neurons in Craig's paper. Maybe I'm just not normal."

I could feel him standing very quietly behind the door. "There's no such thing as normal, Emily," Aeden finally said. "It doesn't exist in nature, and it's not in your destiny to be alone. That's absurd." He paused here, and then said, in a gentler voice, "Can you at least think about it?"

"It won't change a thing, Aeden," I said, but my heart was thumping. "Even if I thought about it for a hundred years it wouldn't change anything. I'm not cut out for that kind of life, the one you will eventually want to have. It's not in me. It never has been in me. And I don't want you to be unhappy."

"I wouldn't be unhappy with you, Emily," Aeden said, sounding upset at me. "You're wrong about that."

"Please go away," I said.

"Listen to me, Emily." I imagined him stubbornly leaning his forehead against the door. "I'll make a deal with you. I'll stand out here for five minutes. Starting now. If after five minutes you haven't opened the door I'll take that as a no. I'll leave and you'll never hear from me again, I promise you."

I began to count the seconds in my head, but I soon lost track of time and gave up counting, and after only a few moments I heard him stepping away from the door, and his footsteps receding down the hallway, until I stopped hearing him altogether, and realized the five minutes had passed. And in that moment I felt a longing so deep for Aeden, for all the years in which I hadn't known him, hadn't known that someone like him was out there in the world, it almost hurt to breathe.

I yanked the door open and flew outside, into the hallway, and I thought I could see him standing some fifty feet away from me, by the fire exit. And then I realized it wasn't just a thought: He was really there. His back was to the exit sign and he was facing the east side of the hallway, where I stood in my nightgown with my hair pulled back away from my face. Aeden started toward me, determinedly, and when he reached me I leaped into his arms. "I'm going with you," I said.

"I love you, Emily," he whispered in my ear.

I pressed my nose to the crook of his neck and a thousand revolving doors locked into place, like molecules in a crystal sheet. From the depths of my heart I saw the old yellow school bus again, but more clearly and distinctly than ever before—if indeed I had ever really seen it. Haltingly the bus approached a snowed-in street corner and came to a full stop. The doors creaked open and a small child in a winter coat appeared at the top of the stairs, and began to descend them. A woman, also wearing a coat, stood waiting for the child at the bottom of the stairs, and for an instant, while the fantasy lasted, she and I were undeniably one and the same.

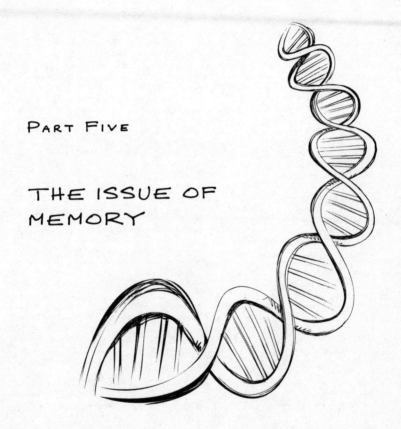

PART FIVE

THE ISSUE OF
MEMORY

CHAPTER 27

O FTENTIMES, MORE OFTEN THAN I CARE TO AD-
mit to myself, I wonder about the kind of life
I would have had with Aeden had I stayed with him the following
morning, instead of going back to the lab.

I imagine flowers in a vase, though I don't care very much for
flowers, and a dog running unleashed in some small and un-
tended but beautiful yard. I imagine informal gatherings with
friends at our place and a child or two running barefoot in the
house—children miraculously sprung from the recombination
of our genes, his and mine.

I see us drinking ballooned glasses of Baileys by the fireplace
in winter, and in summer lying in the sun on outdoor patio chairs
with the scent of our sweat soaked into the flimsy fabric of our
clothes and the day advancing at a lazy pace, and I wonder what
it would have been like to grow old together; I wonder if Aeden
would have been happy with me, and I with him, and I ask myself
whether it was worth it to have returned to the lab the next day.

After we embraced in the hallway he lifted me in his arms
and carried me back to my dorm and pushed the door open with
his knee. I laughed out loud, feeling like a bride in a movie. Or

maybe I laughed because I was aware of dwelling at that moment in some high-altitude place for a limited period of time, and the image of the bride came later, years later, when I began flying across the country to give talks on smell and catching unwanted glimpses of silly movies on the backs of people's headrests. I don't know.

In my dorm the smell of detergent had reached my bed by the window. Aeden lowered me to the ruffled cream sheets, kicked off his shoes, and sat down next to me. We kissed and talked, and kissed and talked some more, almost too seriously, in retrospect, about the small country house we were going to rent in Massachusetts, and after a while we took our clothes off and made love under the sheets while outside time seemed to freeze.

Short of pancake mix and various permutations of coffee there was nothing to eat in my pantry, so we phoned China Fun and ordered vegetable rolls and stir-fried rice with chicken and a side order of steamed spinach. The food was delivered at midnight to my doorstep, in brown paper bags with white napkins and plastic forks and enough fortune cookies to go around a conference room, though I don't think we opened even one.

We ate at the small table by the window, where hours earlier I'd sat examining images of olfactory neurons. The screen had long since dozed off, and while Aeden chewed and swallowed and spoke to me about the logistics of leaving (we would drive up north over the weekend, crash at his friend's house in Boston, look for a place on the outskirts of Cambridge, within twenty miles of Neurogen) my attention kept wandering every so often to the spiraling galaxy of my screensaver, as though I were stepping out of my skin and seeing for the first time the vastness of everything, the many roads I'd never noticed, or dared to see. How I've hated coming across that screensaver throughout the years.

After we ate and discussed the future we got back into bed, and eventually fell asleep. But a few hours later, when it was not quite yet daylight outside, I awoke to a troubling dream. A dream I've never been able to reconstruct except to say that in the midst of it my eyes snapped open as if someone had shouted my name. Something was wrong, something about our results didn't add up. I stared at the ceiling, unable to make sense of the dream, or to understand what was wrong, and then I quietly rose out of bed and got dressed. When I returned from the bathroom Aeden was still sleeping. In the neutral light of dawn his face was bluish pale and his eyelids veiny. I could see his eyes, under his eyelids, moving in a way that made me imagine he was racing in his dream, running away from someone or something, and yet his breathing was gentle and unbroken, almost peaceful. I stood by the bedside in my jeans and hooded sweater, watching him sleep, and then I turned away and left.

———

WHEN I REACHED THE BUILDING IT WASN'T QUITE SIX A.M. THE lab was gloomy and deserted, but the door to the main room was open, and I could see light spilling into the hallway. I was half expecting to find one of the other postdocs in the lab, or a graduate student dismantling an overnight experiment, but instead I found David, standing in his lab coat by the sink, capping an assembly line of water-filled jars with little black screw-on lids. It was a brainless, thankless task, reserved for the floor technicians and unpaid summer students and also, when there was no one else around to do the job, for research technicians like himself. Watching him, before he noticed me there, I felt sorry for him, and for all the hours of work he'd poured into the database. Mainly, though, I felt guilty for what hopes he'd no doubt entertained of having his name on a paper.

"How are you, David?" I asked at last.

He raised his eyes to mine. "I'm fine, Emily. And you?"

In my bay I changed into my lab coat and stood staring at the spreadsheet on my desk, at the date of birth, gender, ear-punch specifics, and olfactory bulb phenotype of the mice we'd analyzed. The data was shatteringly clear, but in the back of my head was that feeling I'd had in the dream, of the world turned upside down; the sense and certainty of there being something I'd overlooked and needed to do.

I was still struggling to make sense of the dream, to make sense of why I was there, when I heard a rasping little sound, and turned around to see David standing in front of me, a downcast, apologetic sort of look on his face. I thought he was about to tell me he was sorry about the knockout results, and then saw a white object in his hand. It was Aeden's timer, the one he'd lost. David was holding it practically under my nose, like an offering.

"It was in 309," he said. "On the floor."

Room 309, I knew, was where wild-type mice and a few other strains with normal olfactory bulbs were housed. I noticed the safety clip was broken, but made no move to take the timer from him. Something told me that to take Aeden's timer wasn't exactly what David wanted me to do. "You can leave it on his desk," I said.

"Justin said to give it to you personally," David said.

IN THE COLD ROOM THE AIR STANK OF FORMALDEHYDE AND
faintly of cadaverine—that rotting smell you can sometimes
whiff on the breaths of people with problem teeth. I stood in
the center of the room with my arms wrapped around my chest,
shielding myself from the chilly air and scanning Aeden's over-
crowded shelf for the tray with our heads.

Three doors down, in the imaging room, I sat in front of a
scope and pulled out the vials from the tray and reexamined our
bulbs, one at a time. Nothing had changed, of course. Nothing in
the map of smell was amiss. Hundreds of nerve endings reached
their targets in the bulb reliably, inevitably almost, as though
they had been destined to do so. Nothing lost, nothing gained,
everything normal—too normal, almost.

There's no such thing as normal, Emily. It doesn't exist in nature.

I sat there recalling what Aeden had said, and remembered
what he'd told me once, a few months earlier, discussing science over coffee during one of our late weekend mornings in his
kitchen. That in the bulbs of their knockouts he and Allegra had
spotted a few wandering axons, but in such small numbers as to
render the phenomenon negligible, certainly not publishable.
If this was true for their mice, why wasn't it true for ours; why
weren't there any stray neurons? Why was the map of smell of our
mice so normal-looking?

Almost without thinking, I rose from the chair and left the
imaging room, walking swiftly and mindlessly back to my bay.
David hadn't moved from my desk. When he saw me he said, "A
litter of mice is missing from room 309."

"Aeden might have used them as a control," I offered, despite

the fact that to my knowledge such controls were not required in
our experiment.

"But why six?"

"What's wrong with six?" I countered.

"Wasn't that the number of mice you analyzed?" David said,
unnervingly straightening his eyeglasses.

"How do you know that?"

"It's my job to know these things, Emily. I also know your
knockout litter was under a different label for a week. I'm not a
half-wit. Justin isn't either. He knows much more than you give
him credit for." He looked at me more carefully. "Where is the
missing litter?"

"I don't understand what you're getting at, David," I said—
though a part of me already did. "You're suggesting I analyzed
those mice instead of our knockouts? I took the knockouts out of
room 310 with my own hands."

"How can you be so sure?" David asked me. "Did you regenotype them?" He was smiling now, a thin and embarrassed smile,
as though he'd been waiting for me to come to my senses.

I stepped back from him and left the room, covering the distance between it and the steel door at the end of the hallway at
a limping trot, wanting and not wanting to ever reach it. In the
cold room, the biohazards bin Carlos hadn't yet emptied was
overflowing with mouse carcasses. I knelt on the cement floor,
straddling the bin between my knees, and with the stench of cadaverine pressing into my nostrils began to pull out nylon bags
of decapitated mice. I hadn't dug beyond the surface of stiff bod-
ies when my fingers hit something hard and bony.

There were six mice inside the bag, with their heads intact.
Still, something in me refused to do the math, to make the night-

marish connection between what I was holding in my hands and our knockout mice. It wasn't until David had dissected them and stained their bulbs, until I laid down one of the bulbs on a scope stage and pressed my face to the eyepiece and I saw the surface of the bulb emerge into focus under the harsh bright lights, that the truth came to me, in a searing flash.

There they were, the neurons whose destiny I had altered. Without my gene they did not reach their targets. Instead they wandered open-ended paths, as I had hoped they would, and I had to shut my eyes against the pain.

CHAPTER 28

I N MY DORM A MIXTURE OF COFFEE AND DETER-
gent filled the air with an inscrutable odor I've
often encountered in airports in the early morning, before the
first flights of the day have begun to take off, the sort of smell
that has invariably driven me to head straight to my gate, far
from the crowded food stations and mopped floors.

Two hours had gone by since I'd left him. I hadn't expected him to
still be there, but he was, standing barefoot at the kitchen sink. He'd
made the bed and gotten dressed and dismantled the refrigerator
shelves I'd forgotten to rinse. Two were already drying on Bounty
sheets on the laminated counter. The other one he was still working
on, scrubbing the Ajax off with a brand-new sponge I imagined him
unearthing from the dark cabinet space under the sink where I kept
my few cleaning supplies. On the stove, an espresso contraption I'd
never bothered to use was fizzling with coffee, and there was music
too, jazz streaming softly from my laptop near the window.

I stood by the doorway, looking at him. Pillow marks were indented on his face, two thin lines running like rail tracks down
the side of his left cheek. It occurred to me it was the last time I
would be seeing them on him.

"You should have left me a note," Aeden said, smiling at me from the sink. "I was about to phone you in the lab."

I entered the kitchen and sat down at the table behind him. "David found your timer," I said. "In room 309." Then I said, "Six mice are missing from that room."

Aeden glanced over his shoulder at me and we made eye contact for a second before he looked away. The faucet was still running, but he just stood there, without moving.

"Those are the mice we analyzed, aren't they, instead of our knockouts?" When he didn't reply I continued. "I found our knockouts in the trash. Luckily the bin was still there. Otherwise I would have never found out, right?"

"No," Aeden said.

"The phenotype is dazzling," I said, ignoring his confession. "Certain areas of the map are very nearly destroyed. I'm sure you would be impressed, Aeden."

"The experiment doesn't matter to me, Emily. I was thinking only about you, about us." He was no longer facing the sink. "Nothing else mattered."

"What about what mattered to me?" My voice was quivering.

Aeden came over to the table and sat down next to me. "Your gene will still be here a hundred years from now. But you and I won't. Do you understand me?"

"Right," I said, looking away from him. "I nearly forgot we were supposed to be together. How could I have been so blind?"

"Don't do this," Aeden said, closing his eyes. "Please don't do this to us." When he opened his eyes again tears were streaming down his face. He took hold of my hands.

"Forget the results," he said. "Please, just let them die in the trash."

"That's impossible," I said. "You're asking me to become a different person, to be someone I'm not."

"I'm asking you to choose me, Emily. That's what I'm asking you to do, to choose us."

I saw my sunken reflection in his eyes and heard a voice out in the hallway, and light footsteps skipping past the door. Children actually lived on the floor, on practically every floor of our building, children whose mothers went to the lab every morning and cooked dinner in the evening and made love to their husbands at night and met up with friends over the weekend. I thought about that, about having everything people aim to have in life: a career, family, intimacy, happiness, or the idea of happiness Aeden had painted for me: sharing a house with him where a dog ran wild in the yard, spending the rest of my life with him. Was it so impossible to have all these things, or was it just not possible for me?

"You know what I would like?" I finally told him, standing up from the table.

Aeden dropped his head into his hands, as though he already knew.

———

IN THE LAB HE EMPTIED OUT HIS DESK OF FOUR YEARS IN THE time it takes to fill out a form at the dentist's. Cardboard boxes were already nested like Russian dolls beneath his desk. I had noticed them that morning when I walked into our bay, light on my feet still with that feeling of vastness, never imagining how things would end.

While he packed I stood outside, by the elevators, waiting for Aeden to do what I'd asked him. At last the double doors of the lab split open and Aeden wheeled a cart of boxes past me, into an open elevator. He turned around and looked at me, but I didn't move. I hadn't planned to say goodbye. I didn't want to.

"Emily," he said, ramming his arm between the shutting doors. "Emily, please, is this how you want things to end?"

"No, it's not," I said, wondering if I would ever see him again. "But you've left me no choice." He looked at me for a long moment, until his arm finally went down, and I saw his face vanish.

A day later I walked into Justin's office equipped with images of the bulbs of the mice I'd dug out of the trash and watched him smile with delight as he went over them. To my relief he didn't ask me a single question about Aeden. He conveniently turned a blind eye to the discrepancy between the initial results and those on my laptop screen, and so did David, and so did I, in the end.

At the time I told myself that by not breathing a word to anyone in the lab about what Aeden had done I was being only fair to him, and in fact that was true. But what I never let myself believe, and what was also true, was that I was trying to make myself forget, not so much what he'd done, but what could have been had I never found those mice in the first place.

The following year, working over the weekend at my washed-out, cluttered bench with short strands of DNA designed to recognize potential variants of my gene, David and I isolated from his library a series of gene fragments. I reconstructed the fragments to their full length and incorporated the sequences into a phylogenetic tree of axon guidance genes in my computer and nearly fainted at the sight. A fresh new limb sprouted from the tree, a limb bearing a small family of guidance molecules exclusive to the sense of smell.

It was an exhilarating sight. It was also, in retrospect, the most lonesome thing I've ever seen.

CHAPTER 29

S URFING THE NEUROGEN WEBSITE LAST WEEK IN
my office, I came across a picture of Aeden I
hadn't seen in a very long time. It was late in the evening and
I was sitting at my desk, struggling with the opening of the
Lasker Award acceptance speech. Usually I'm able to string
words together fairly quickly, and with conviction, but on this
particular evening my mind kept wandering. After an hour of
false starts I closed the document and clicked an icon hidden
inside a folder on my screen. The moment I did so I felt a soothing calm wash over me, as if to open the Neurogen website, to
explore it again as I had done in the past was what I'd yearned
all along to do.

The first thing I saw on the web page was the footbridge link-
ing the two unpresuming buildings of red brick across a narrow
stream. Except this time there was a rowboat in the water, with
four would-be employees sitting inside it, smiles on their young
faces and their oars idly held in their hands. I knew it was just an
ad, but I couldn't help but feel a little upset by what it seemed to
me to be misleadingly portraying: that to do science, to give one-
self wholly to the search for truth, is something anyone can do;

that we are in fact naturally born and inclined and even destined to give ourselves to such work.

I thought of Aeden and smiled, imagining that he would have some venomous but insightful and amusing remark about the ad, and then I scrolled past it, with hesitation, to *Scientists* at the top of the page. The list was longer than before, but his name, to my relief, was still there. I clicked on it and before I could inhale, an image of Aeden popped up on my screen—the same photo of the thirty-three-year-old I had first seen when the picture was uploaded on the site eleven years ago. In the picture— which Aeden for some reason hadn't bothered to replace—he was aiming his old inquisitive smile at me: a smile that always seemed to be on the verge of uncovering some important truth. Seeing it again that evening, for the first time in two years, the picture had the feel of a fresh start, a new beginning.

Starting from the time that he left the lab, Aeden had sent me Christmas cards and birthday cards almost religiously each year, and in between them a host of emails telling me how he was and inquiring about my own life: how was academia treating me, where in the city was I living, was I seeing someone, was I happy? The last message I had received from him, some two years earlier, was different, longer and more direct than the others, claiming there were loose ends we needed to tie up and arguing that it really wasn't fair, my silence after nine years. How long could someone hold a grudge, and what was the point? He cared deeply about me, and despite my silence—because of it, actually—he suspected I still cared for him. He needed to see me as soon as possible. Would I be in town over the weekend?

I never answered this letter, or the others. I never even acknowledged receiving the greeting cards either. Though oftentimes I felt strongly inclined to do so. One particular weekend, setting up my lab over the Christmas holidays in a building so empty I could hear the wind outside from the hallway, I spotted, in my usual pile of junk mail, an envelope from Aeden. Inside was a card with a picture of a deer pulling a sled full of packages up a snowy hill dotted with tiny beautiful houses lit from within. The scent of cinnamon rippling from the inside of the card compelled me to open it, and when I did I was struck by the familiar sight of his handwriting, wishing me good luck with my appointment at the Chemical Senses Institute. It was a thoughtful gesture, and I had wanted to email him saying thank you, but didn't. He had tried to interfere with my research, and what had made him think he could do that, decide what was best for me? A few years after that I saw his name on a paper describing neuron regeneration and memory gain in aging mice treated with growth factor proteins. I had been eager to send him a congratulatory note, but decided at the last minute against it. I was still angry with him for trying to take my fate into his hands. But more than this, I was inexplicably angry with myself.

Sometime soon after Aeden's last letter, the one in which he'd asked to see me, his correspondence had suddenly stopped. I missed hearing from him, but I was also secretly relieved not to have to grapple with the memories, up until a year ago, when I began to wonder in earnest why Aeden was no longer communicating with me.

The question was one I'd been mulling over for several days, along with memory. How is it that neurons in our hippocampus, that seahorse-shaped area of the brain where memories are stored, persist in firing off their signals? Or more precisely, why do they? Why does the brain insist on rehashing what the mind would rather forget?

I was thinking about this when Giovanna burst into my office, startling me to a standing position. "What can I do for you?" I asked, aware that those had been Justin's words to me when I'd appeared in his room unannounced. Somehow they'd stuck.

"Can I talk to you for a moment?" Giovanna said, darting a look at Aeden on my desktop screen. Her breathing was labored, and her face disarmingly pale.

"Is it time?" I asked, glancing at her belly, over which her lab coat strained.

But Giovanna shook her head and the next thing I knew I was following her down the hallway of the lab to the imaging room: a crammed, airless cubicle where biological specimens are observed at up to two-thousand-fold magnification, a place where truths are revealed, the wanted and the unwanted, and people's futures are very often decided—whether they will stay on in research or leave, find something else to do with their lives.

Jutting out of a petri dish, on the lit stage of a scope, was the olfactory bulb of a mouse belonging to the strain she had made, genetically designed to model a congenital form of anosmia that is present in humans. Anosmia caused by injury to the head is often incurable, especially in adults. But smell loss due to other causes might still be curable.

Our goal was to determine if enhanced expression of certain pathfinder genes in these animals could help rewire their olfactory bulbs and restore the sense of smell they'd been born without. I wasn't particularly hopeful about the experiment. I never am. But then skepticism can grow on you like an addiction.

I sat down in front of the scope and lowered my head to the eyepiece. In the canned, stale air of the room I could feel the warmth of Giovanna's body next to mine, and the reassuring tumescent odor of sloughed skin I've come to associate with maternity. What did I look like to her, I wondered, with my new farsighted prescription and the recent invasion of grays in my hair, the cumulative effect on my waistline of a steady diet of coffee and muffins? She'd been in the lab for, how long, close to two years? In that time she'd met a man she'd liked well enough to move in with, engineered a mouse strain existing in no other lab in the world, and brought a baby to near full term. In the two years it had taken me to summon the courage to revisit Aeden's picture on a web page, Giovanna had made something out of nothing, created life where none had existed.

The bulb was veiled in a haze. I played with the focus knob of the scope and the fog lifted, revealing nerve endings spatially segregated into groups, coursing defined pathways in the bulb, ultimately coalescing onto targets called glomeruli. In one small cross section of the bulb I counted more than a dozen glomeruli, and imagined the axons that innervated them firing their signals: fragrant, woody, pungent, chemical, minty. How many of these odors and others might these animals be able to smell now?

"I'm dying here."

I had momentarily forgotten that Giovanna was next to me. For many months she had been waiting for this moment, and the moment had finally arrived—the only one she would probably care to recall in years to come. Before she knew it she would write a paper describing how pathfinder proteins restore networking in the olfactory bulbs of mice with congenital anosmia; she would publish this paper and apply for funding to expand her research; and maybe, if she really wanted it, and family allowing, she would have her own lab. And though I've somehow ceased to be impressed by these kinds of achievements, and though I've been through a similar song and dance with several other very dedicated and extremely fortunate postdocs in my lab, I raised my face to hers, and, smiling in the darkness, said, "The results are remarkable," whereupon Giovanna flung her two strong arms around my neck, nearly knocking me out of my chair.

I guess that's when I knew that I had forgiven Aeden; when I told myself that the memory of our last time together was not the one I wanted to go on living with.

CHAPTER 30

Y ESTERDAY I RECEIVED AN EMAIL FROM AEDEN—
the first in just over two years. His message came in response to the email I sent him last week, inviting him to the Lasker Awards ceremony that will take place here in New York tomorrow, and letting him know that in my acceptance speech I would acknowledge his contribution to the pathfinder project. Aeden's letter was brief, and whether he planned to be at the ceremony was unclear. But overall I was more than pleased with it.

> Dear Emily,
>
> It's nice to hear from you. As you know I've thought of you often. I miss that period of my life. I haven't been doing a lot of traveling lately but it so happens that I'm on my way into the city today for a meeting, and would love to see you.
>
> My sincere congratulations,
>
> Aeden

I had been going over the opening sentence of my speech and feeling dissatisfied with it, when his email arrived. It was early in the morning, earlier than most people in my lab, in most labs in the building, get to work, so I had the luxury of being able to sit there at my desk and read and reread Aeden's email while some highly cognitive area of my brain acknowledged the knot taking shape in my stomach.

Some three hours later, after a string of email exchanges in which Aeden and I defined exactly where and when to meet, I was out in the street, dodging buses and taxis and pedestrians in the snug-fitting dress and high-heeled shoes I keep in my office closet and wear to conferences and for the occasional blind date. On my way out of the lab I had stopped by the bathroom to take a close look at myself in the full-length mirror, and ended up standing in front of it a good deal longer than I had anticipated, realizing sadly that the image in the glass did not align with the one in my head. I looked older than I'd thought, or had cared to admit: thicker around the waist and with more than just a few grays tainting my red hair, and more than just a few sunspots on my face, despite my forty years of relative enclosure. To make matters worse, there seemed to be a downward tilt to the right-hand corner of my mouth that gave my face, when I wasn't smiling, an almost tyrannical air.

I'd been with a number of men since Aeden, but unfortunately there had been none about whom I could tell myself, as I had once told myself about him: *Maybe it could be, would be, if I allowed it to happen.* I don't mean to imply by this that I was entertaining the hope of getting back together with him, but it would be a lie to say that I absolutely wasn't.

Our meeting location was the Nectar diner on the southwest corner of Madison Avenue and Eighty-Second Street—the same place I'd fled into years ago with Allegra's hairclip. I've been there many times since: weekend mornings, mostly, before the brunch crowd takes over, when I will sit at one of the booths in the front with a stack of research papers and catch up on my reading over breakfast and coffee. I like the modestly cheerful atmosphere of the place, and the jar by the cash register filled with peppermint spheres. I like how the door chimes every time someone steps in, and how the sun across the windowpanes un-covers cracks and stains and all sorts of imperfections on the otherwise smooth white tiled floor.

It was I, of course, who suggested that we meet at the Nectar, knowing that I would feel more at ease in a place I knew well. I arrived a good ten minutes early, and was relieved to ascertain that Aeden was nowhere in sight, and that moreover the place was almost empty. I walked over to the nearest booth and sat down facing the door. The idea was to see him before he could see me, to not be taken by surprise.

Behind me, in one of the larger booths by the restrooms, a group of elderly people sat soberly chatting over leftover strips of bacon and refilled cups of coffee, waiting for the stores and mu-seums to open. Directly in front of me, across the aisle, a young woman was obliviously chatting on her phone. Parked next to her was a stroller, and inside the stroller a sleeping infant with a pink cap on her head. I thought of Giovanna, and wondered if she too would soon be spending her mornings in diners and cafés, eager for a taste of freedom. I didn't know whether she was ex-pecting a boy or a girl, and had never thought to ask. The fact that her life would soon be tethered to that of another human being had dwarfed for me the question of gender.

The infant stirred in her sleep and kicked off her blanket. Watching her I had a sudden fear that she would wake up and start

to wail and that my initial encounter with Aeden would be ru-
ined, but then her mother, as if she'd been reading my thoughts,
stood up from her booth and wheeled the stroller toward the cash
register. "I understand," she kept saying into the phone, even as
she paid her bill. "No. I do. Seriously." Her insistence made me
wonder if she really did understand what the person on the other
end of the line was trying to tell her. If anyone ever really under-
stands anyone else. The thought of this, paradoxically, gave me
hope.

I heard a chime, and looked over to the door to see a tall, thin
man holding it open for the mother: Aeden. I stood up and he
caught sight of me and mechanically smoothed back his hair, or
what remained of it, and when the woman had stepped into the
street with her stroller he let go of the door. For a moment we
stood awkwardly gazing at each other, until Aeden walked over to
me and we lurched into each other's arms.

"I've missed you, Emily," he said, tightening his hold on me.
"I have missed you so much."

"So have I, Aeden." My face was pressed to his chest. I thought
I could smell on him something sour and faintly medicinal, like
aspirin, but wasn't sure.

Eventually he released me and stepped back, and we stood
there, within arm's reach, looking at each other. I saw dark circles under his eyes and it occurred to me that something was
wrong. My biggest fear during the last two years had been that
Aeden had contracted lung cancer from all his years of smoking
and was terminally ill, and I didn't know it.

"Do you still smoke?" I asked, trying not to sound alarmed.

Aeden shook his head as though I'd asked him if he'd killed
someone. "Quit," he answered. "A long time ago."

"I'm happy to hear that," I said.

At the booth the waiter stood two tall glasses of water on our table and slapped down a pair of menus. I opened my handbag and pulled out a guest pass to the Lasker Awards ceremony: a long rectangular strip of paper that looked more like a bookmark than an actual pass to anywhere.

"What's this?" Aeden asked.

"Your ticket to the awards ceremony."

Aeden took the ticket from me without a word, as though it were a napkin I was offering him to clean his mouth with, and slid it into his shirt pocket. "I'm assuming David Hobbs will be there?" he asked across the table, with a hint of sarcasm.

"Him and his wife," I said.

"I guess he made it into medical school after all."

"He just finished his residency," I offered, meaninglessly adding, "I'm very happy for him."

"What about the asshole? Will he be there too?"

"Justin is retired," I said. "I walked into the lab last month and thought I'd walked into a war zone. They're in the process of erecting another lab, and there's someone new in charge, a young couple, with a child. Anyway, I don't know that he will be there."

"I'm glad," Aeden said. "About Justin retiring, I mean. He was a terrible lab head."

"The responsibility was maybe too much for him," I said, wanting for some reason to defend Justin. "And he always had other interests, aside from science."

"I bet you he's locked up in some hotel room with a *Playboy* as we speak," Aeden said, paying no heed to my comments. He made as if to laugh, but didn't. Instead he held my gaze for a long moment. His eyes were the same indeterminate gray I remem-

bered, in which I'd once seen myself reflected. "You don't look a
day older, Emily."

I smiled at him. "You're just saying that."

"I'm not just saying it. I mean it."

"I look much older than I did the last time we saw each other,
Aeden. I know I do."

"Not to me you don't. To me you look the same."

I opened my mouth to ask him what I'd had in mind about
memory, but I didn't want to spoil the moment. "I keep up with
your work," I said. "I've read all your papers on memory. It's im-
pressive, what you've accomplished in just ten years."

"You never wrote me back," he said. "For nine years, not a
peep from you. Not even to let me know you were reading my
letters."

"It was silly of me not to. I'm sorry," I said.

Aeden looked at me with concern. "What's going on in your
life? Personally, I mean."

"Between my responsibilities in the lab and the traveling,
I don't have much time for a personal life, as you can imagine.
What about you?"

"I'm married," Aeden said.

My eyes dropped to his hand, and I saw on one of his fingers
the wedding ring I hadn't noticed earlier, or hadn't wanted to notice: a plain band of silver. "That's nice," I said. And smiling with
effort, "How long have you been married?"

"Eighteen months."

For an interminable moment neither of us spoke. I could feel
him staring at me, and couldn't bring myself to meet his eyes.
I felt that if I just continued to sit there and stare beyond his
shoulder, at the sun crashing through the windowpane behind

him, the moment would soon pass. Given enough time it would be behind me, like most other moments of my life.

"There is no meeting," he said. "I drove all the way here just to see you, Emily. I should have done it years ago. I wanted to see how you are, and to apologize for trashing your results."

"Our results," I said, making an effort to speak casually.

"Ours, yours, there's no excuse for what I did. I've thought about it for years, how you and I would be together now if I hadn't done what I did."

I mustered a laugh. "No, we wouldn't," I said. "I'm genetically hardwired to be alone. You know that about me."

"No, you're not," Aeden said. He sounded annoyed. "We had this conversation a long time ago, across a shut door, remember?"

"I remember," I said, managing a smile.

"What did I tell you?"

"You said it wasn't in my destiny to be alone."

"And what did you do, shortly after that?"

"I opened the door and stepped outside and there you were, waiting for me."

"You agreed to go to Cambridge with me, to give it a shot, didn't you?"

"I did," I admitted.

Aeden looked at me with conviction. "It will happen again," he said. "With someone else."

"It won't," I said. "It will never happen again."

He sat back in his chair, studying me from under knitted brows. "It will," he said. "One day. I guarantee it." As if to convince me of this he dug into his coat pocket and pulled out his phone and handed it to me. I lowered my eyes to the screen and found myself staring straight into a pair of light gray eyes like

Aeden's, except noticeably slanted. There was an overwhelming calmness about the gaze, a quiet tranquillity that made me think of someone only half-formed, not yet fully conscious of himself or the world. Not quite yet human.

"He's beautiful," I said, handing him back the phone. "How old is he?"

"Twenty days," Aeden said proudly. "Twenty-one, actually."

"Now I understand why you look so tired." The sour smell of earlier, I realized, was curdled milk.

"You actually know his mother, Emily. Remember Ginny?"

I could hardly believe my ears. "Ginny from the lab?"

Aeden gave me a sobering smile. "I guess you do remember her."

"I remember we used to make fun of her. I remember she used to wear so much perfume it made her smell like a skunk. I remember . . ." I wanted to also remind him about what he'd said, how he would be bored out of his mind with her, but I found I didn't have the heart to. "You even came up with a theory to explain the phenomenon. How did you end up with her?"

"She changed perfumes," Aeden said, trying to humor me, but the smile had faded from his face.

"I'm not amused," I said. "Does she still play the oboe?"

"Not lately, but she'll get back to it soon. I hope."

"She sure could carry a tune," I said, and immediately regretted it. What did I know about music, after all, about art; what did I know about anything other than my narrow field of expertise? "What about her bloodhound?" For some reason I couldn't bring myself to say his name. "How is he?"

"Smokey?"

"Yes. Smokey." Suddenly I wanted to cry.

"Gone," Aeden said. "He was old even back then, ancient, really, for a dog."

Unable to bear it any longer, I grabbed my purse and stood up. "I need to leave," I said.

"I was hoping to have breakfast with you," Aeden said, sounding disappointed.

"I have a meeting I forgot about, with a student." My voice was shaking.

He nodded understandingly at me and stood up, catching on to the lie. "I'll walk you out," he said.

———

AT THE REGISTER AEDEN PAID FOR THE TWO COFFEES WE HADN'T consumed and stood joylessly watching Galina (platinum-dyed hair and now working the register after twelve years) process the payment. There was a sad air of conformity about him standing there, slightly stooped in his beige coat, that made me wonder if he was genuinely happy. It seemed impossible to me that he was, that he could ever truly be himself with Ginny, but then who was I to say that he wasn't?

The jar with the peppermint candy I'd never tried was right under my nose. I brought one up to my mouth and cracked it open between two molars. A minty odor wafted retronasally up to my brain, deflecting the immense sadness that had begun to descend on me. I was transported back to my childhood, to my father summoning me with a roll of Life Savers across our den window to join him in the yard, where he was planting vegetables. At the beginning I'd refused, on account of the smell of grass, but then I'd joined him, and we had ended up having a fine day together. It seemed as though a similar window of opportunity had presented itself just two years earlier, with Aeden's last letter, the one in which he'd requested, demanded almost, that I forgive him. But I hadn't.

Outside I could feel Aeden studying me across the sunlit air as I gazed toward the street, assessing the unebbing flow of traffic. After two failed attempts to flag down a cab I stepped around him and wordlessly began heading south. I could feel Aeden following me but didn't turn around to look. What I wanted was to be alone, to allow the grief to sink in and phone him later to apologize for my behavior.

I had nearly reached the corner when I felt his hand on my shoulder, and saw him waving a piece of yellow paper in front of me. It was his guest pass. "I can't go, Emily," he said. We were standing only inches apart, and yet his voice felt as faint and distant as if he were miles away. "I can't make it to the ceremony. And even if I could, it wouldn't be a good idea. I honestly think my being there would only spoil your evening."

"It wouldn't," I said. "It absolutely wouldn't." But I could already see the futility of Aeden's presence at the awards ceremony, and with crystal clarity the vital years of our lives behind us, dissipated like smoke. The tears I'd managed to suppress rushed to my eyes, and I told him what I knew I'd wanted to tell him all along, and had never told anyone before him, except maybe my father. "I loved you, Aeden," I said. "I loved you."

"I loved you too, Emily," he said. "I still do."

"I wish I had known it," I said. "That you were marrying her." Aeden smiled at me. "Would it have made a difference?"

"I don't know," I said, shaking my head. "I wish I could say yes, but . . ." I tried to swallow. The tightness in my throat was unbearable.

He tucked a strand of hair behind my ear. "I'll come visit you again some other time, when it's over." By "it" I knew he meant the awards ceremony.

I nodded. "I would like that, Aeden. I really would."

Before losing myself in the nearest side street, before the tears streamed down my face and the world became a blur, I glanced behind me and saw him standing where I'd left him, and then he was gone. Ahead of me was a narrow path dotted with brownstones and caged trees with their branches static in the windless sky. I wasn't sure where the street led out to, and didn't care.

_____

CHAPTER 31

WHENEVER I SIT DOWN AT A SCOPE TO OBSERVE the olfactory bulbs of mice made in my lab, I often find myself reflecting on the courses of people's lives. I see nerve endings swerved off their paths, reaching places in the map of smell different from those they were genetically predetermined to reach, and I think about destiny, and I ask myself if it exists as such. I get to wondering if there's a single place each one of us is meant to arrive at or if there is no such place, and destiny does not exist: we simply make our way as we go along.

Yesterday, after I parted from Aeden and randomly turned into that narrow side street on the southwest corner of Madison, I found myself staring across Fifth Avenue at a building I slowly came to recognize as the Metropolitan Museum of Art. I'd been there only once, nearly twelve years earlier, and had not returned since.

I crossed the avenue and climbed the steps to the entrance of the museum. In the lobby I purchased a ticket, and after a few false leads on the cavernous first floor was finally able to locate the wide staircase leading to the second.

Upstairs, beneath tall opalescent ceilings, a guided tour was in session, but it was a relatively small and noiseless group made up predominantly of elderly people. I shuffled quietly past the torso they were huddled around and made my way into a large open room, and across it, through a maze of similar rooms. My feet hurt from managing high heels and my throat was swollen with the knot I was still fighting to keep from unraveling. It took several rounds of tortuous wandering to locate him, but I finally did, in room 827, cornered on a narrow wall between a small bright red painting and a very large one of a woman in a black dress who looked like she was about to break out in song.

He seemed to be observing me with his troubled dark eyes from his desk, but in truth he was looking at the artist who had portrayed him, more than a hundred years ago and thousands of miles away. Garshin's portrait was not, as I'd once thought, a self-portrait, but it was the notion of one that had made me uncover the unique nature of my gene. Without this insight it was unlikely that I would have ever tested its function and identified an entire family of similar genes, and without Garshin's striking resemblance to Aeden it was unlikely that I would have ever stopped to observe him in the first place, or that I would have observed him long enough to have had the insight. And if I hadn't stopped to observe him, and if I hadn't discovered what I did, Aeden would have never misled me, and we might have very well ended up together. It was as if these two things, Aeden and the discovery, could never coexist with each other: as if only one of the two had been meant to be and I had made my choice.

A few feet from where I stood, there was a low wooden bench. I walked over to it and sat down. And there, just like that, I began to cry. Not in the quiet way in which I'd cried in the street, but a choked, muddled sob punctuated by high-pitched screeches not unlike the squeals of a frightened mouse, a cry as primitive-sounding and primal in origin as the sense of smell. Two other people were in the room with me, a girl in her twenties and a man about my age. They'd been standing with their backs to me, discussing a painting hanging somewhere to my left, and now they kept throwing worried looks in my direction. I held a hand over my mouth, but it was useless. The tears kept rolling down my face, and my throat emitting that terrible sound. I could not remember ever crying this way before, and I could not stop.

The tour group I'd seen earlier came flocking into the room, past the bench where I was sitting, and gradually disappeared into a connecting room. *It is important that you see this before you die,* I imagined their guide telling them, and somehow that thought was able to calm me. I scavenged my handbag for a Kleenex and dried my eyes. Of the two people who had been in the room with me, only one remained, standing very still in front of the painting he'd been examining, with his face practically touching the canvas now. I thought I could see a magnifying lens in his hand, and protruding from the back pocket of his jeans a flat-edged head, similar to a spatula. A suggestion of turpentine seemed to emanate from where he was, but the smell could have come from anywhere: the entire room was one gigantic oil painting.

The man stepped back, away from the canvas, and inserted the instrument in his hand (it *was* a magnifying lens) into his other pocket. Then he glanced over his shoulder at me and we acknowledged each other in silence. Something about his face was very familiar, but it wasn't until he was standing over me, blocking my view of Garshin, that I realized who he was.

"I hope you're feeling better," he offered kindly, his chunky arms folded around a visibly protruding belly.

"Thank you," I said. "It wasn't my intention to make a scene."

He waved a hand in the air. "People are always inspired to tears in this room, don't ask me why." He was smiling genially at me, displaying the gap between his two front teeth, discolored now with age. His face was stockier than I remembered, and his blond hair streaked with gray.

"I'm Emily," I said. "And you're John, right?"

He squinted at me, evidently not remembering who I was. "Have we met before?"

"Twelve years ago," I said. "In this room, in front of that portrait." I pointed at Garshin, but John didn't turn his head around to look. He didn't have to. Garshin's was the only portrait in the room. "We exchanged a few words about it and then I left and I haven't come back again since." I thought of telling him about his input in my discovery, but it felt out of place, and for some reason insignificant. "You offered to show me a self-portrait of van Gogh. I don't know if it's still here, or whether you have time. You're obviously working. But I'd love to see it if you have a few minutes."

———

JOHN IS AN ART RESTORER IN THE MUSEUM, AND HAS A WORKSHOP on the top floor: a small, busy space similar to the imaging room in my lab, except crammed with canvases instead of microscopes. After showing me the van Gogh painting and the workshop, he led me downstairs, to the first floor, past a byzantine hall with terra-cotta bowls encased in glass, through a pair of glass doors, and into a vast interior courtyard flooded with light. The glass ceiling was beautifully mirrored on the marble floor, and above our heads I could see white clouds roaming the sky.

We walked past the line of tables where twelve years earlier I'd sat having coffee, and around a bronze naked woman with one leg raised in the air, deftly pointing her bow and arrow at us. "Diana," John said, and with engrossing finality, "goddess of the hunt."

"Thank you for the tour," I said, embarrassed. I hadn't expected him to go out of his way to show me around, and he had. "It's very kind of you."

"We're just getting started," John said, and smiled so earnestly at me I had to look away. I had a vague impression that he was flirting with me, but wasn't sure whether he liked me or merely felt sorry for me after what he'd witnessed, or both.

When we got to the entrance of the American Wing he held the door open for me—a glass door with a darkly tinted, reflecting surface. "Is it true what they say about sharks?" he asked. "That they can detect a drop of blood a mile away?"

"I don't know anything about sharks," I told him, and stepped past him, into the gallery, where I let myself be led along a checkered floor to the entrance of the exhibit room in which John had said were some nineteenth-century portraits he wanted to show me.

We were about to enter the room when I recalled my father telling me how every species and every individual in a species is locked in its own sensory world, and this gave me an idea. I had planned to say, in the opening of my acceptance speech tomorrow, that in the brain there's a map of smell. But now I would change that. I would start off with something less scientific, something my father used to tell me long ago, before I thought of becoming a scientist, before I ever dreamed of discovering anything even remotely related to smell: *Smell is an illusion, invisible molecules in the air converted by you into cinnamon, cut grass, and burning wood.*

It was here, or maybe we were already standing inside the exhibit room, that I told John I needed to leave. It was getting late, I explained, and there was something important I had to do.

"Now?" he asked me, a hand raised to his chin, looking a little taken aback. "You need to leave now, this very second?"

"I'll come by next week," I said. "I promise." Then I did something strange, and entirely unexpected. I opened my handbag and pulled out the pass Aeden had returned to me and handed it to John. "I hope you can make it."

John regarded the yellow stub in his hand with an almost childlike interest. "I look forward to being there," he said.

That's when I turned from him and, quickening my steps, began to make my way back alone, to the entrance of the gallery. I had nearly reached it when I saw a middle-aged woman advancing uncertainly toward me from the other side of the door, a trusting look in her amber eyes. I thought she was about to ask me for directions, but it was just me.

T HE RESEARCH PROJECTS AND FINDINGS IN THIS book have no exact analogues in scientific literature. Their plausibility is based on established scientific principles and documented gaps in knowledge of the late 1900s and early 2000s. The steps carried out by Emily and Aeden to make the knockout mice are founded on existing techniques.

While Emily's discovery of a new family of axon guidance genes is fictional, her source of inspiration is real: the portrait of writer Vsevolod Mikhailovich Garshin hangs in the Metropolitan Museum of Art, in room 827.

ACKNOWLEDGMENTS

I AM INDEBTED TO MY STELLAR AGENT, KIRBY KIM, for his enormous enthusiasm for this book, and to my talented editor, Katherine Nintzel, whose input in the work was transformative.

My gratitude to Joey Coyle and Gabriela Hidalgo Zaragoza, who read and critiqued early drafts of this novel, and to writing mentors, friends, and family who read excerpts of the book in its conception and provided precious feedback: Rita Gabis, Carol Goodman, Russell Working, Clint McCown, Connie May Fowler, Xu Xi, Ellen Lesser, Joel Rothman, Ivan Rothman, Melina Patris, Jennifer Cohen, Leah Kaminsky, Leonor Hidalgo Coyle, Deborah Kashanian, Sharon Khazzam, Alexandra Ainatchi, and Maria E. Arreaza.

Several of the science-related aspects of this project were facilitated by specialists who generously took the time to answer my questions about anosmia, bioinformatics, and color vision: Leslie J. Stein and Beverly Cowart from the Monell Chemical Senses Center, Ryan Taft from Illumina, and Steven R. Ali from Manhattan Vision Associates.

I would also like to thank Brenna English-Loeb from Janklow & Nesbit, who reviewed the submitted manuscript of this book, and the fabulous team at William Morrow HarperCollins that brought the book to life: Vedika Khanna, Laura Cherkas, Nyamekye Waliyaya, Linda Sawicki, Aryana Hendrawan, Julie Paulauski, and Amelia Wood.